He pe
darkness. ...

It couldn't be. He was hallucinating out of some mixture of desire and anger. She couldn't possibly be here, walking alone, through the storm.

"Conor." The way she said his name, so filled with joy and relief, yet also with mingled apprehension, shattered any thought that she was an illusion. This was a flesh-and-blood woman, soaking wet, buffeted by the wind, yet still incandescently beautiful.

And infuriating.

He got out of the car and stalked toward her. His voice rose above the wind, hard and iron-edged. "What in hell are you doing here?"

Nickie took a quick step back. She wasn't afraid, precisely. Just cautious. The storm tore at him, but he seemed oblivious to it, standing there tall and indomitable, his chiseled features tautly drawn and his eyes alight with emotions she didn't care to recognize....

Dear Reader,

If you have children, it's back-to-school time for them—and that means more reading time for you. Luckily, we've got just the list of books to keep you enthralled, starting with *One Last Chance,* the fabulous American Hero title from Justine Davis.

And the rest of the month is pretty terrific, too, with titles from Suzanne Carey (a bit of ghostly fun to get you set for the Halloween season), Nikki Benjamin, Maura Seger, Clara Wimberly—an Intimate Moments newcomer whose Gothic novels may be familiar to some of you—and star-in-the-making Maggie Shayne. (Look for her next month, too—in Shadows.)

I'd also like to take a moment to thank those of you who've written to me with your thoughts and feelings about the line. All of us—editors and authors alike—are here to keep you reading and happy, so I hope you'll never stop sharing your comments and ideas with me.

So keep an eye out for all six of this month's books—and for all the other wonderful books we'll be bringing you in months to come.

Yours,

Leslie Wainger
Senior Editor and Editorial Coordinator

PRINCE CONOR

Maura Seger

Silhouette® Intimate Moments™

Published by Silhouette Books New York

America's Publisher of Contemporary Romance

SILHOUETTE BOOKS
300 East 42nd St., New York, N.Y. 10017

PRINCE CONOR

Copyright © 1993 by Seger Inc.

ISBN: 0-373-07520-0

First Silhouette Books printing September 1993

All the characters in this book have no existence outside the imagination of the author and have no relation whatsoever to anyone bearing the same name or names. They are not even distantly inspired by any individual known or unknown to the author, and all incidents are pure invention.

®: Trademark used under license and registered in the United States Patent and Trademark Office and in other countries.

Printed in the U.S.A.

MAURA SEGER

and her husband, Michael, met while they were both working for the same company. Married after a whirlwind courtship that might have been taken directly from a romance novel, Maura credits her husband's patient support and good humor with helping her fulfill the lifelong dream of being a writer.

Currently writing contemporaries for Silhouette and historicals for Harlequin and mainstream, she finds that writing each book is an adventure filled with fascinating people who never fail to surprise her.

Chapter 1

Dan Philips was the first person to see Nickie Chandler the day she came home to Block Island. She stopped at his gas station for a fill-up. He took one look through the plate-glass window and hustled out to take care of her himself, instead of letting his sister's boy do it as usual.

Nickie was sitting behind the wheel of a red convertible, honey-blond hair blowing in the early autumn breeze. She was tired, having driven for five hours, and had a whole lot on her mind.

When Dan ambled over, she glanced up, said "Hi," and asked him to fill it up. On an afterthought, she added, "Oh, and could you suggest some place where I might be able to find a room?"

A few weeks before, during the tourist season, that wouldn't have been a problem. But now most places were closed down.

"You could try the Gull's Rest outside of town."

"The Woodwards' place?"

Dan nodded. "That's the one. Hey, how did you know that?"

"I used to live around here."

He squinted at her more closely. Sure enough, she did look familiar now that he thought about it, but the gas was almost pumped before the penny dropped.

"You're not . . . Nickie Chandler?"

She smiled, but there was a touch of wariness in the large, aquamarine eyes. She handed him a twenty and told him to keep the change. "I'm not?"

He was still staring after her as the convertible disappeared down the road.

Nickie settled back again behind the wheel. She didn't usually give flip answers to anyone and it bothered her that she had now. She was more on the defensive than she'd expected.

All around her the golden, sand-strewn world looked weirdly familiar yet different, like something seen in a dream. As though somebody had come along and rubbed off the rough edges of the place and its people. Except obviously that wasn't what had happened. Any rough edges that had come off were strictly her own.

She'd left Block Island a frightened, defiant, determined young girl. She'd come back a woman. It didn't hurt that she'd built a good life for herself, but mostly she was just plain grown up. Which meant that her perspective had shifted.

Her fingers flexed slightly on the steering wheel, releasing the tension in them. Maybe this wouldn't be so horrible, after all. Less the confrontation she'd feared and more a gentle summing up and putting to rest of the doubts that had haunted her since that long-ago day when she'd left.

Left Block Island and Conor McDonnell.

Her smile faded. She'd be lying if she tried to tell herself that she was no longer worried about how she'd react to Conor after all this time. And how he'd react to her.

But there was nothing to say she'd have the chance to find out. He probably didn't even live on the island anymore. She'd left, why shouldn't he have done the same?

Relieved by the thought, she put her foot down harder on the accelerator and let the wind empty her mind.

Dan didn't waste any time. Ever since he'd had that accident on the motorbike back in '72, he'd limped pretty badly. But he still managed to get himself into the office and onto the phone before Nickie was a mile down the road.

The first person he called was Donna Woodward.

"Nickie Chandler's back and she's coming over to your place looking for a room."

"*What!*" When Donna got excited, her voice rose to a high pitch exactly like the one chalk made when

being scraped on a blackboard. She also tended to take
any kind of surprise personally, as though fate was
trying to pull a fast one on her.

"What're you talking about, Dan? Everybody
knows Nickie Chandler's down in Connecticut somewhere, writing those trashy books. Besides, if she ever
did come back here, why wouldn't she just stay at her
mother's place? They've still got it even though Patty
Chandler hasn't lived there in ages now."

Ordinarily, her response would have set Dan back.
But he knew he had the upper hand this time so he just
ignored her.

"Fine, don't believe me, but I'm telling you, Nickie
Chandler's gonna be knockin' on your door inside of
five minutes." That said, he hung up the phone with
a good, hard *klunk*.

Donna sat on her chintz settee by the living-room
window and wondered if there was any chance Dan
was right. Nickie Chandler, of all people. Now that
would really be something, not that it could be true,
but if it were... boy, oh, boy....

She would have been only too happy to speculate—
at length and in juicy detail—but her front doorbell
was ringing. Chalk one up for old Dan. Nickie Chandler was standing right there on the front porch.

Donna pretended to be surprised. She reeled back,
clasped her hands to her ample bosom, and smiled a
little tearfully. "Oh, my...don't tell me...it isn't...is
it? Little Nickie Chandler."

Donna wasn't a very good actress. And Nickie remembered her well enough to be wary on principle

alone. Still, she gave her a nice smile. They didn't cost anything, far as she could tell.

"It's nice to be remembered, Mrs. Woodward. Dan Philips said you might have a room for me."

As if there was a snowball's chance in hell of Donna turning her away. Still, they went through a little back-and-forth.

"Well...let me see now. You know the season's over and I've let my help go. But since it's you..."

"Thanks," Nickie said as she picked up her bag and gave a meaningful glance in the direction of the shiny keys hanging behind the front hall desk.

It was a good thing she did, otherwise Donna might have stood there all day looking at her. Not that it wouldn't have been worth the effort.

Nickie had been pretty as a girl, but she'd tried to hide it, dressing down, keeping her hair scraggly, using no makeup. Taller than average, she'd tended to slump. But all that had changed. Now she stood proudly, a graceful woman casually but attractively dressed in jeans and a turtleneck sweater that complimented her willowy, long-legged figure.

Donna's mouth pursed. "I do hope you'll be comfortable," she said. "We're just a simple little place."

"I'm sure it will be fine," Nickie said, and took the key from her hand.

Half an hour later, she had unpacked her bag and settled in as much as she was going to be able to. That done, there was no excuse not to go back outside and have a look around. But she got no farther than the

bottom of the stairs when Donna stuck her head out
from the front parlor.

"There you are, dear. I thought you might be feeling a little hungry after that long drive so I fixed a few
sandwiches. Why don't you come in here and relax for
a while?"

Relax? More likely sing for her supper, Nickie
thought wryly. Donna was about as transparent as
they came, but she couldn't find it in her heart to
blame the woman for being inquisitive. Wasn't everyone at least a little curious about other people?

Besides, gossip was a two-way street.

A short while later, Nickie was seated in the parlor,
nibbling on a roasted chicken sandwich with dill may-
onnaise on thinly sliced white toast and doing her best
to satisfy her hostess's appetite for information, within
reason, of course.

"I've come back to close up my mother's house,"
she said. "Eventually, I'll do something about selling
it."

Donna nodded gravely. "It's for the best, dear. I'm
sure Patty is much better off wherever she is now."

"I hope you're right. She died last month."

Donna gaped. She blinked hard several times and
cleared her throat. "I'm terribly sorry."

"So was I," Nickie said quietly. "She had the best
possible care, but she'd lived a pretty hard life and it
caught up with her in the end."

"That's true," Donna murmured. "Your father
dying in that accident when you were just a baby was

awful, but your mother did try to pull things together. It just never seemed to work out for her."

There was a great deal Nickie could have said, about a community that had turned its back on a young, frightened woman, about the men who had exploited her and the women who had condemned her. But she kept it to herself the same way she always had—except for that one time with Conor when it had all come out.

"So how have things been here?" she asked, determined to change the subject. "I've been out of touch. Maybe you could fill me in?"

Just as the sun rose and the wind blew, asking Donna for gossip was like appealing to an irresistible force of nature. You did it and then jumped back, hoping you wouldn't get sucked into the undertow.

"Well . . ." Donna moistened her lips, settled herself more comfortably in her chair, and locked eyes with Nickie.

"You mean you don't even know about Frank McDonnell's bank going bust and the family losing all its money?"

Whatever Nickie had expected, it wasn't this. Struggling to hide her shock, she said, "No, as I said, I've been out of touch. All of it?"

"Every last dime. Seems he'd been embezzling funds for years and the government finally caught up with him. No S&L bailout for them. The bank had to be sold and rumor had it Frank was about to be arrested, 'cept he had a massive heart attack and died before they could get to him. That left Conor to pick up the pieces."

"What about his mother?" Nickie asked in a low voice. Dimly, she was aware of Donna looking extremely satisfied by the effect she was having.

"Didi took herself off to Florida at the first sign of trouble. She'd divorced Frank a couple of months before he died and had married some retired stockbroker down there. We haven't seen hide nor hair of her since."

"So Conor...?"

Dolefully, the older woman shook her head. "Poor boy. He had everything in the world, didn't he? And now he's got nothing. Whereas you..."

The point couldn't have been more obvious. Wait long enough and the world turns upside down. The golden prince is cast down and the little match girl becomes a queen.

Except that this wasn't a fairy tale. This was real life and Nickie was sitting right smack in the middle of it.

"I see...." she said slowly. "That certainly *is* a surprise...."

Donna sat back and smiled. She didn't protest when Nickie excused herself a short time later. She had phone calls to make.

Chapter 2

Gull's Rest was at the end of what passed for a main street. There was a road, right enough—it wrapped around Water Street and headed out toward the dunes—but the buildings that dotted it were mainly survivors from the previous century, when the island had been a popular vacation spot for Victorian families.

Nickie thought about taking the car, then decided against it. After almost five hours of driving, she needed a walk. The day was brilliantly clear. Along the rolling dunes for as far as she could see hung the golden light of early autumn. A brisk sea breeze cooled her cheeks and made her dig her hands more deeply into the pockets of her jacket.

She walked along slowly, in no great rush to get anywhere and resigned for the moment to simply taking in her surroundings. Memory flowed through her. Tomorrow, she'd start work on her mother's house. But first she needed to gather her strength.

Haley's Seafood Restaurant was closed for the winter but she could see in through the windows. It didn't look much different from when she'd gotten her first job there a dozen years before, waiting tables twelve hours a day, seven days a week. The pay had been lousy but the tips were good. She'd managed to squirrel away quite a bit that long ago summer.

Not much farther down the road was the Seadrift Hotel, also closed. She'd worked there, too, in between her shifts at Haley's. To this day, she could clean a bedroom and bath in her sleep. After all, she'd done it that way often enough.

Ruefully, she shook her head. She still put in twelve-hour days and had been known to work weeks on end without taking a break. But it was work she loved and felt lucky to have. That made all the difference.

Her long, slender legs carried her farther away from the main part of town, around the bend toward the beach. Ahead, the ground rose to form a small hill commanding a magnificent view of the land and water. Crowning the hill was a glistening white house surrounded by ancient pine trees and looking like a jewel set down directly by the hand of a generous deity.

Conor's house.

Nickie stopped on the side of the road and stared up at it. Her throat tightened. For a moment her vision blurred. She blinked fiercely, denying the tears that threatened to fall.

Conor.

She couldn't think about him, not when she was feeling far too fragile to cope. Later, maybe tomorrow, when she'd had a chance to accustom herself, then she'd think about him. But not now.

Please, not now.

Memory—contrary, elusive, formidable—refused to be denied. It beat against the walls of her resistance like a great, magnificent bird demanding the freedom to soar.

All around her the golden light gleamed. She breathed a long, shaky sigh and turned away from the house. But not before she saw the sign on the wrought-iron gates.

For Sale.

So Donna had told her the truth, or at least a reasonable semblance of it. The house that had sheltered four generations of McDonnells was being sold. Moreover, if the condition of the sign was anything to go by, it looked as though it had been on the market for some time.

Not really too surprising. Plenty of people wanted houses on Block Island, all right, but not the huge behemoths that required so much upkeep. It was surprising, though, that a developer hadn't snapped it up for the land alone.

She was still staring at the sign, trying to get used to what it represented, when she heard hammering coming from the far side of the house. Hesitantly, she took a step forward. The wrought-iron gate was unlocked. It creaked open at her touch.

Trying very hard not to think about what she was doing, Nickie walked up the driveway. White gravel crunched under her feet. The lawns had been mowed recently, but the garden looked overgrown even for this time of year. Several of the trees needed pruning, too.

The hammering continued, growing sharper as she came around the back of the house. She stopped, looking straight ahead.

A man was up on a stepladder repairing a shutter that had blown loose from a ground-floor window. He wore a plaid shirt, khaki slacks and work boots. His thick chestnut hair was disheveled and slightly long. Seen in profile, his features were hard, rugged, uncompromisingly masculine.

And achingly familiar.

Nickie must have made some sound although she was unaware of it. The man turned suddenly. His big, powerfully muscled body jerked when he saw her.

"Who...?" he said hoarsely.

She stood silent and unmoving, unable to make a sound or turn away. As though time itself had frozen and she with it.

"Nickie?" His tone was incredulous, his expression even more so. Slowly he put down the hammer and lowered himself from the ladder. His eyes never left her as he walked the short distance across the lawn. He stopped several feet away and stared at her warily.

"Nickie."

"Yes." A quick, unconvincing smile left her face feeling like stiffened clay. Awkwardly she said, "I guess I'm trespassing but I was walking by and saw the sign...."

"Walking by...?" he repeated, still trying to come to terms with her sudden and utterly unexpected appearance. Although he was convinced now that she was real, he still had the sensation of a man who finds himself in a strange and bewildering dream.

Abruptly he asked, "What are you doing here?"

Nickie hesitated. She didn't want to get into it. Her gaze slid away from him. "I'm closing up Mom's house. She died last month."

His dark, slanted eyebrows rose above features that looked suddenly haggard. "I'm sorry."

"She'd been very ill for a long time."

"Yes," he said quietly, "I know."

Nothing more needed to be said. Conor had known, better than anyone else.

"I won't be here long," she said.

A stab of pain darted through him. The thought that she could flit back into his life after so long, arouse such unwanted emotions, and then vanish again left him aching.

Of course, he knew about her success. He'd seen her by accident one night on a talk show. She'd looked beautiful then, but even more so now standing before him in the opulent light, straight and slender and proud, her chin tilted defiantly and her eyes an odd mixture of defiance and pain.

"I see," he said slowly.

She swallowed hard, knowing she should go right now, turn her back and walk away. Knowing that she couldn't.

"Conor...I was sorry to hear about what happened. It was all news to me, I've been out of touch for so long. But it must have been terribly hard for you."

His eyes narrowed, hiding his thoughts. "I survived," he said shortly.

She could see that—and more. The man she remembered had still been part boy. His features had been softer, more relaxed. He'd smiled readily, with the assurance of one who has always been welcomed and successful. His height—he was several inches over six feet—had been the same, but now he seemed to have grown into it, his shoulders and chest having broadened and the whole of him giving the impression of enormous, coiled strength.

Beside him, she felt suddenly, startlingly, vulnerable, a sensation she had not experienced in a very long time. Deep within her jacket pockets, her hands trembled.

"The house..." she said suddenly, desperate for any distraction, "...it's beautiful."

"It's been in better shape," he said frankly. For a moment he hesitated, as though unwilling to commit himself any further. Finally he relented enough to add,

"I try to get out here every couple of days, but that's not the same as someone actually living in it."

"Why don't you?" she asked, unable to repress her curiosity.

"It's too big for one person. Besides, I prefer living closer to where I work."

That at least answered one question she hadn't been willing to ask—was he married? Apparently not. Not that it mattered. The quiver of relief she felt was mere reflex, nothing more.

"I didn't realize..." she said, only to stop herself in time. She'd been about to say that she hadn't realized he'd be working, which was ridiculous under the circumstances, if not actually insulting.

With the family fortune gone, of course Conor would need a job. He was certainly intelligent enough to do anything he set his mind to. Besides, she recalled he'd been planning to attend Harvard Law School. Most likely, he'd gone to work for one of the top-flight Boston firms and spent his days in genteel surroundings practicing corporate law.

The only thing wrong with that picture was that the man before her didn't seem to fit it. He was too big, too hard, too... primitive somehow to imagine sitting behind a desk in a white shirt and suit being clever and amicable for powerful clients.

"Whereabouts are you these days?" she asked. "Boston?"

He shot her a quick, surprised look. "Not any more often than I can help it. I'm not much of a city person."

"Then where...?"

"I've got a place in the reserve," he said, referring to the portion of the island set aside as a nature refuge. "It's convenient to the area I'm studying for a survey on coastal erosion."

Nickie shook her head, feeling all at sea. "You're not a lawyer?"

His brow furrowed. "Of course not. What made you think that?"

She hesitated, unwilling to make any mention of that summer ten years before. As it turned out, she didn't have to. Conor remembered without any prompting.

"Harvard Law. I'd almost forgotten that I'd planned to go there." He smiled ruefully. "Things didn't turn out quite the way I expected."

Which by all accounts was putting it mildly. She managed a faint laugh. "Life does have a way of throwing us curves, doesn't it?"

His glance was quick, perceptive, all-encompassing. It swept over her in an instant and was gone, but not without her feeling it to the very center of her being.

"You seem to have made the most of them," he said quietly. There was no resentment in his tone, only simple honesty.

"I've had some luck."

"And you've worked hard. You must have."

"It hasn't been so bad," she demurred. "Well...not all the time." A smile flashed across her heart-shaped face. "Actually, I've enjoyed it a lot."

He believed her. She had the look of a woman who had met great challenges and triumphed over them. He knew that feeling, having encountered it himself in his own work. It was something they had in common despite everything else that separated them.

The tension he had been feeling since first setting eyes on her eased a little. Whatever had once existed between them, some resonance of it must still remain. He was wary of her, but he also felt an impulse to friendship that was difficult to deny.

He was not an impulsive man. Hard experience more even than basic character had made him cautious. That was an asset in his work, where infinite patience and meticulous attention to detail were essential requirements. But in personal relationships, it could be a liability.

He had to remind himself that the past was past. Besides, they had both been very young back then and surely youth deserved forgiveness simply for its own sake.

"I'm almost finished here," he said quietly. "Would you like to get some dinner?"

Chapter 3

The Clamshell Café down by the beach was one of the few places that stayed open year-round. It was popular with the locals as well as the few off-season tourists—hardy souls that they were—who made it over.

That evening, however, business was slow. Norm Kincaid was standing behind the bar, wiping it down with a wet cloth while keeping time in his head to the cool, sweet tune belting out of the stereo.

Norm was a rhythm-and-blues man, a sixties hippie who had never dropped more than halfway back into society. He'd inherited the Clamshell from his uncle and had managed to kee___ going through a combination of genuine hospitality and pure serendipity.

He was also just about the only person on the island who paid absolutely no attention to what other folks were doing. Either he didn't notice or he didn't care. Whichever, when Nickie and Conor came in, Norm did no more than give them a vague smile and sweep an arm toward the empty tables.

"Sit anywhere you want," he said, then thought to add, "Want a beer?"

"Two," Conor said after a nod from Nickie. They made themselves comfortable in a booth toward the back. An awkward moment of silence followed.

Nickie fiddled with her paper napkin and tried hard not to stare at Conor's large, burnished hands resting on the table so close to her that she had only to reach out the slightest distance to touch the blunt-tipped fingers, the dusting of golden hair, the hard, callused palms...

Abruptly, with a faint edge of panic, she asked, "This survey you're doing on coastal erosion, how did you get interested in something like that?"

Conor shrugged. He was silent while Norm set the beers and a couple of menus in front of them. When he'd shuffled off, Conor said, "I reached a point where I stopped taking things for granted. I'd lived here all my life, but I'd never really understood how beautiful the island is, or how vulnerable. When it finally dawned on me, I went back to school, got a graduate degree in microbiology, and signed on with the state environmental protection agency. They set me up doing the coastal survey."

Nickie wanted to ask if he'd put all this in motion
before or after his father's bankruptcy, but that
seemed too personal under the circumstances. Instead she contented herself by asking, "How long have
you been at it?"

"A couple of years now. Before that I was out on
the west coast, doing something similar around Seat-
tle."

So the decision not to follow his pre-ordained path,
not to become a lawyer and enter politics, must have
occurred independently of the disaster that befell his
family. For the briefest instant she wondered if it could
have had something to do with her and with what had
happened between them. Quickly she put that thought
aside.

Norm came back and took their orders. Classic
Lena Horne soloed on the stereo. Outside, the wind
was picking up. It whispered around the corners of the
café and made the windows rattle softly. But inside, all
was warmth and comfort.

Until the door flew open and a man strode into the
café.

He was tall, about the same height as Conor, and
big in a way that suggested a football player gone soft.
His ebony hair was ruffled by the wind and his square,
blunt-featured face looked reddened. He glanced
around quickly, ignoring Norm as his gaze settled on
Conor and Nickie. Without hesitation, he walked toward them.

"I thought that was your car outside, McDonnell," he said as he stopped beside the booth. "Aren't too many wrecks like that on the road."

Conor refused to take the bait. He merely glanced at the man and shrugged. "Something you want, Mulloney?"

"Damn straight, there is." He paused, his eyes narrowing. Abruptly a smile flashed across his broad face. "You can start by introducing me to this lovely lady."

Without waiting for Conor to do so, he turned to Nickie. "I don't believe we've met. I'm Ed Mulloney, Mulloney Development, and you're . . . ?"

"Nickie Chandler," she said automatically, though she made no attempt to take the hand he offered. After a moment, he withdrew it but continued to stare at her approvingly.

"Well, now," he said, "to tell you the truth, I thought that's who you might be. Kind of hard to forget a face like yours, 'specially after it's been all over TV and the newspapers."

"Hardly all over," Nickie murmured uncomfortably. She was only too well aware that Conor was sitting back, observing the encounter with what looked like a mixture of amusement and disdain. Whoever Ed Mulloney was, Conor certainly didn't seem to consider him much of a threat. Or, more likely, he just didn't care if somebody else put the moves on Nickie.

That thought was too bittersweet to be entertained for long. Trouble was, there didn't seem much else to concentrate on. Ed Mulloney was beaming at her, virtually demanding her attention with the misplaced confidence of a man who presumes that his approval is both sought and appreciated.

Not that he was unattractive. He had the rough good looks of the so-called black Irish with ruddy skin, bright blue eyes and midnight dark hair. Moreover, he had a certain charm—part practiced, part genuine—that comes from an honest interest in other people, if only to the extent that they can be used. Nickie guessed that he was in his mid-thirties, about the same age as Conor and a few years older than herself.

There was an aura of affluence about him visible in his elegantly tailored suit and gleaming white shirt. By comparison, Conor looked positively uncivilized, a roughneck in jeans and a work shirt that had both seen better days.

Yet Nickie had no doubt which of the two men she preferred. The question never even entered her mind.

Nor, apparently, did it occur to Ed, who benignly assumed that any woman presented with such a choice would see which side her bread was buttered on in no time flat.

He gave her another quick, approving glance before turning his attention to Conor. "You've been ducking me long enough, McDonnell. My offer on your place isn't going to stand forever. What's it going to be, yes or no?"

"Have you changed your plans?" Conor asked quietly.

Mulloney's flush deepened. "You know damn well I haven't. White elephants like that aren't worth spit these days. It's the land I want."

As though appealing to an impartial observer, he turned to Nickie. "You can't do better than Mulloney Development. We use the best architects, materials, you name it, no corners cut. And the results can't be beat. Every year people are falling over themselves to give us awards. A Mulloney project is tasteful, refined, it's got class. There's absolutely no reason not to jump at the chance to sell to us."

"Except there's already been far too much development on the island," Conor interjected. He didn't raise his voice or indicate in any other way that he was less than perfectly calm, but Nickie sensed how tightly he was holding back.

Instinctively, in an effort to defuse the situation, she said, "The McDonnell house is so beautiful, it would be a shame to pull it down."

Ed sighed as though he, too, regretted the loss. "That's progress, Nickie. What counts is giving the most people possible the chance to enjoy the good life and that includes having a second home on the island."

With a pointed glance at Conor, he added, "Some people seem to think that chance ought to belong strictly to the silver spoon set."

A slashing grin crossed Conor's face. "I turned in my silver spoon some time ago. If I wanted it back, I'd sell you the property and clear out. But I'm not going to do that, Mulloney. Sooner or later, you'll get that message."

If the sudden look of rage that crossed his face was anything to go by, Mulloney had gotten the message—loud and clear. Nickie's stomach tightened. For all his surface gentility, he was clearly not accustomed to being crossed. Especially not by a man he thought ought to be panting to be rescued from the financial mess he'd inherited.

"Sooner or later, you'll come to your senses, McDonnell," he said. "Just don't expect me to be standing around waiting when you do."

With a quick nod to Nickie, the developer banged out of the café, making the metal soda sign on the door all but pop off. Behind him, he left a fog of unanswered questions and unspoken thoughts.

Into it Norm plopped two bowls of steaming clam chowder. Nickie picked up her spoon but left it hovering over the bowl. She stared at Conor. He looked as imperturbable as ever, but private knowledge gained so long ago under such different circumstances told her otherwise.

Quietly she asked, "Do you have any alternatives to Mulloney?"

He shot her a quick, searching glance. "If I say no, are you going to suggest I sell to him?"

She smiled gently. "Aside from it not being any of my business, I've never had much interest in lost causes. It's clear you've made up your mind about him. Now is there anyone else you can sell to or isn't there?"

He sighed and gave her a grin that made him look suddenly boyish. "Let's just say I'm not exactly being knocked down by offers."

"Other developers?" she ventured carefully.

Conor's head shake was emphatic. "No way. They're all the same as Mulloney. Fact is, some are a lot worse. His developments actually aren't as bad as they could be. The problem is just what I said—the island is being overbuilt. The entire ecological system here is threatened simply because there are too many people in too small and fragile an area. I'm not going to contribute to that by making yet one more piece of land available to the bulldozers."

He spoke quietly enough but his absolute commitment to what he was saying was unmistakable. In the face of it, Nickie could only wonder how the privileged, sheltered boy she had known had become so strong and unselfish a man. By contrast, the changes the years had made in her seemed less profound.

She was still, for instance, powerfully attracted to him.

The realization had come to her slowly as she watched and listened to Conor. It came seeping up through the layers of her consciousness, brushing aside all resistance, to explode, fully formed, into her mind.

The ripples of that explosion were still coursing through her when Conor reached out and laid his hard, burnished hand over hers.

Chapter 4

The sudden look of concern, almost of fear, that washed over Nickie's delicate features prompted Conor to reach out to her. Instinctively, he sought to comfort and protect. But the instant their hands touched, a far different feeling seized him.

His hazel eyes darkened. Beneath his hand, Nickie's seemed absurdly delicate. He could feel the fine texture of her bones and the melting softness of her skin.

Touching her, he became aware of a faint, enticing perfume tantalizing the outer reaches of his senses. He had always been particularly sensitive to odors both pleasant and unpleasant.

From childhood, they had been the trigger for memories of all sorts. To this day, he had only to smell

the dry, sweet scent of Arrowroot biscuits to be cata-
pulted back into his nursery.

Nickie's scent unleashed a far different sort of rec-
ollection.

Years before, he had thought her the most desirable woman alive. All unknowingly, she had become
imprinted on his mind and heart to such an extent that
every woman who came afterward was judged against
the standard she'd set.

He had never again encountered the same hot,
sweet, piercing yearning they had known together.
Indeed, he had come to believe that it had never been
anything more than an illusion.

Now he knew he had been wrong.

"Nickie?"

"Yes?" Her voice sounded unnaturally weak, but
he heard it. He took a deep breath, fighting for control, and even managed a smile.

"What else would you like for dinner?" he asked as
he carefully removed his hand.

In fact, she had no appetite at all, at least not for
food, but she wasn't about to tell him that. Instead
they worked their way through a couple of burgers
before gently but firmly declining Norm's cheesecake
of which he was inordinately proud but which nobody else could digest.

It was dark when they left the café. The wind had
picked up, turning the air from pleasantly cool to
outright cold. Nickie shivered as she turned up the
collar of her jacket. She was glad that Conor's Jeep,
decrepit though it might look, warmed up quickly.

"Where are you staying?" he asked her as they drove. When she told him, he laughed. "How is Donna these days? Still the same?"

"Let's just say she hasn't lost her taste for gossip."

He didn't comment, merely nodded and stared straight ahead into the darkness. Which led her to wonder about something that hadn't occurred to her before.

As the daughter of the town drunk, she'd been the object of gossip from her earliest days. But whatever talk there had been about the McDonnells had always been respectful. That must have changed when the truth came out about Conor's father.

She couldn't help but wonder how he'd handled being on the receiving end of the same kind of nastiness she'd always had to deal with. It couldn't have been very pleasant for him, yet he'd stayed to take it when a whole lot of other men would have fled.

"Donna's not alone in this town," he said quietly, his eyes on the road. "Most people around here like to talk. Sometimes they go a little too far, but on the whole they're decent enough."

Ten years before, Nickie would have disagreed with him. But time had given her a different perspective. She was no longer the frightened, desperately proud young girl she'd once been.

"I suppose," she murmured, "it's all just a way for them to keep in touch with each other. But it used to make me feel so ashamed when I knew they were talking about Momma and there was nothing I could do about it."

She must have been tired to say that. It was the last thing she'd intended.

Conor sensed her surprise. Gently he said, "You must have figured out by now that they were genuinely shocked by her behavior and wanted to help. They were just clumsy in the way they went about it."

"She needed help," Nickie admitted. "After Dad died she simply fell apart. I tried to get her to see a doctor, somebody, but she wouldn't go."

She broke off, wondering why she was saying so much. But then, it had always been absurdly easy to talk to Conor. There had always been a rapport between them that she had never encountered with anyone else.

"I wish..." he said, then hesitated. With a faint, self-deprecating shrug, he went on, "I wish I'd been more sensitive to what you were going through. All I saw was what you'd already made of yourself—a beautiful, intelligent, extremely desirable girl. I never glimpsed what was going on beneath the surface until it was too late."

Nickie's throat tightened. She knew exactly what he meant by too late, exactly the moment he must be thinking of, and she couldn't bear to have it come between them now.

As lightly as she could manage, she said, "Well, that was all a long time ago, wasn't it? There's no point dwelling on the past."

Hardly the most original observation she could have made but it served its purpose. Conor gave another quick, accepting shrug and let the matter drop.

When he pulled the Jeep up in front of Gull's Rest, Nickie thought she saw a curtain flutter in the living room window. Conor saw it, too, and his mouth tightened. "Looks like Donna's on the job as usual."

Nickie tried to make light of it, though she was feeling a strange, tantalizing disappointment at their lack of privacy. Which was the surest sign she could have that her wits were deserting her.

Before they could leave entirely, she opened the Jeep door and got out. Conor followed and came around to meet her on the other side. They stood, looking at each other, heedless of the wind riffling their hair and edging its way beneath the folds of their clothing.

Uncertain of what to say or do, Nickie fell back on tried-and-true courtesy.

"Thank you for dinner," she said, and held out her hand.

Conor looked at it for a moment before he smiled wryly. He took her hand, shook it very properly and was about to let it go when some imp of recklessness took possession of him.

Holding her eyes with his, he raised her hand to his lips. She stiffened and tried to pull away, but he held her just firmly enough to prevent that.

No longer smiling, he turned her hand over and slowly, deliberately, touched her palm with his mouth.

The effect was electrifying for them both. Nickie swayed toward him as her knees weakened. Conor caught her around the waist but the movement was automatic. He was far too immersed in the taste and feel of her to be more than half aware of what he was doing.

For a timeless moment, the intervening years rolled away and they were as they had once been: young, heedless and passionately in love. Nothing else mattered. They had only to remain lost in a memory of exquisite pleasure to make it true.

Until a car backfired in the distance and they were abruptly returned to reality.

Conor raised his head shakily. His gaze was storm-ridden as he stared at Nickie. She was pale, the only color in her face centered in her glorious blue-green eyes and the full, moist rose of her mouth. He could feel the tremors racing through her and knew that he was no steadier.

At the window, the curtain fluttered again. With a deep sigh, he said, "You'd better go in."

She didn't understand him at first. When she did at last she flushed and pulled away. "Good night," she said as she hurried up the steps.

Thankfully, the front door was unlocked. She stepped inside and shut it behind her without looking at Conor again. To do so would be to dangerously test her resolve.

She didn't stop until she was safely within her own room. Downstairs, she could hear Donna darting out into the entry hall an instant too late. The woman's disappointment was almost palpable, but Nickie ignored it.

All her attention was focused on the sound of the Jeep pulling away in front. Not until she could no

longer hear it did she relax enough to take a deep,
shaky breath.

Her heart was beating wildly and every inch of her
body felt painfully alive. All her careful defenses, so
well guarded over the years, had crumbled. A well of
emotion opened beneath her.

She felt herself falling into it even as she sat down
abruptly on the bed. Head in her hands, golden hair
spilling about her, she did the only thing left to her.
The thing she most despised.

She wept.

Chapter 5

In the morning Nickie felt considerably better. The storm of tears had washed away a good deal of her tension with the result that she'd slept more soundly than she had in a long time. Yet it was only a little past dawn when she awoke.

For a time she lay under the covers listening to the cry of the gulls out over the bay. To her, the sound had always seemed a siren's call bidding those who heard to come dance between sea and sky. As usual, she found it irresistible.

She left the bed and dressed quickly, pulling on teal blue running pants and a matching sweatshirt. A quick dash of soap and water on her face, a swipe with her brush through the heavy mane of her hair and she was ready.

She tiptoed down the stairs and let herself out the door. If the snores from the back bedroom were anything to go by, Donna was sleeping in. Outside, the day was fresh and alive.

A block or so from the guesthouse, she felt sufficiently warmed up to start running. At first she kept the pace light, more interested in enjoying herself than in getting a rigorous workout.

She'd started running a couple of years back, right around the time it had stopped being fashionable. Walking had become the thing to do, but she still found that she liked the action of running. It took her out of herself and stilled the usual clamor of her mind.

Or at least it always had before. This morning was different. Deliberately, she picked up the pace, stretching herself, demanding and getting more from her body. Her lungs dragged in air, her muscles moved smoothly; she should have felt totally in control.

Instead she felt curiously on edge, as though she was trying to run from something that couldn't be escaped.

It didn't take a blinding intellect to figure out what that might be. All the time she was running, she was thinking about Conor and what had passed between them the previous day.

Although she couldn't remember her dreams, she had the feeling they had been rich and deep, and that he had figured prominently in them. That thought brought a flush to her cheeks that had nothing to do with the run. She slowed down, coming to a halt on a bluff overlooking the bay.

After the fact, she realized that she had come to a spot that had been her favorite as a child. Then she had taken every opportunity to slip away from the misery of her home life to find refuge in the peace and purpose of nature. How long had it been, she wondered, since she'd done anything similar?

With a deep sigh, she settled down on the ground strewn with pine needles and tufts of sea grass. The gulls were busy feeding out on the bay. She watched the quicksilver flash of their wings until something else caught her eye.

A small boat was moving shoreward. It came swiftly, propelled not by a motor but by the long, steady strokes of the man at the oars.

Nickie shaded her eyes from the rising sun. Silhouetted against it, massive and dark, she could make out an achingly familiar shape.

Conor.

Despite the cool morning air, he was dressed in a short-sleeved T-shirt and shorts. It was easy to see why. The boat was a sleek, low racing shell that cut through the water with seemingly effortless grace.

The impression was deceptive, as she saw when he came closer. With each stroke of the oars, the powerful muscles of his arms and thighs corded from intense effort.

Nickie watched, unwillingly fascinated by the evidence of male strength and skill. His rhythm was steady and sure, each stroke of the oars being carried through to its ultimate length before being smoothly pulled back to begin again.

The shell slipped past her vantage point, changing her perspective and allowing her to see what this steady rhythm did to the taut cords and sinews of his back. Unbidden, her fingers moved as though she were touching him, feeling for herself the enormous strength he harbored.

Abruptly she made a choking sound and jumped up. What was wrong with her? She was no adolescent to be mooning about a man because he happened to look good. Surely she had long ago passed that stage.

Yet with Conor she felt absurdly young, as though the years had not happened and she was once again eighteen, filled with an almost frightening intensity of passion and willing to believe that anything she desired could come true.

It had, hadn't it? She had achieved everything she wanted. Nobody would ever again call her poor little Nickie or look down on her because of circumstances she couldn't help.

So why was she so curiously discontent, so riddled by a sense of incompleteness that she had come back to this place where she had sworn never again to be?

Angry at herself, and at the situation, she turned her back on the bay and broke into a hard, demanding run. This time it worked. She managed to keep her mind mercifully blank until she reached Gull's Rest.

As expected, Donna was waiting anxiously for her return, but Nickie managed to elude her by pointing out her immediate need for a shower.

Her luck held when she came back downstairs. She managed to slip out without being seen. Once in the car, she hesitated, but only briefly. She had come to the island to perform a painful but essential task. It was time to begin.

The cottage where her mother had lived was on the shore road leading out of town. It was a ramshackle place built in the 1920s and it had been allowed to pretty much go downhill ever since.

Nickie sat in the car, looking at it for several minutes. Now that she was actually here, she was surprised by how small the cottage looked. It had loomed larger in her memory.

With a shiver, she remembered how the winter wind had torn through the uninsulated walls, how the ancient space heaters they'd owned had provided scarcely any warmth, how she'd had to do her homework sitting in front of the oven.

There were other memories, as well—of pleading with her mother to stop drinking, stay home, take better care of herself, be more like the mothers of other girls. Somewhere along the line—maybe at thirteen or fourteen—the pleas had stopped and the shouting began. She became almost unbearably angry at her mother, until the rage had threatened to consume her.

None of it—not the tear-filled begging of a frightened child or the fury of a deeply wounded adolescent—had made any difference at all. Her mother was her mother. Patty Chandler seemed intent on following a predestined course that nothing and no one could alter, and whose end lay in only one place, the bottom of a bottle.

Now she was dead and buried, the mourning done. At least officially. But the past lingered, still demanding to be put to rest.

Slowly, Nickie got out of the car. She walked up the path to the front door. The porch was missing several planks. She had to step carefully.

The key stuck. For a moment she thought she wasn't going to be able to get in and felt unashamedly relieved. But with a little more pressure, the lock gave.

A musty, damp smell assailed her as she stepped inside. She flinched and had to resist the impulse to back away. It was more than two years since her mother had lived in the cottage, but Patty Chandler had adamantly refused to allow it to be cleaned out. Although she must have realized that she would never leave the nursing home, where she had finally agreed to be admitted, she had been unable to give up her ties to her former life.

Nickie had gone along with her, partly because she simply didn't want to have to fight it out, but also because she couldn't help but sympathize with her mother at least to some small degree. As the final months of Patty's life had dragged out, Nickie had told herself that the cottage could wait.

But no longer. Until it was done, that part of her own life would never really be finished. If she was going to move on into the future, she had to put the cottage and everything it represented truly in the past.

Grimly she set about opening windows. Although the day was bright, she also turned on every lamp. Yet shadows lingered around every corner. She took a deep breath, summoning courage, and decided to start upstairs.

The cottage had two bedrooms. One had been Nickie's, but she had taken everything she cared to from it when she'd left ten years before. Whatever remained Patty had long since disposed of. That left her mother's own room.

Nickie paused at the door. The room was exactly as she remembered. The bed was even unmade, the covers tossed back. Clothes lay over the battered wicker chair that stood in one corner. Nearby was an equally worn dresser. An ancient, lace-fringed runner covered the top of it. Brown circles stained the fabric.

Quickly, she opened windows, trying hard not to breathe too deeply. The room smelled of dust and mold, but beneath it was the lingering scent of the perfume her mother had always favored, a strong, sensual scent Nickie would forever associate with her.

The fragrance gave her a headache. She pushed the windows open as far as they would go but still had to force herself to turn back to the room.

A pile of magazines lay by the bed, mostly the movie variety with a few crumbling supermarket tabloids thrown in. There was an empty glass on the floor beside them, a dark sediment in the bottom.

She would need boxes, Nickie thought, forcing herself to concentrate. Some of the clothes still hanging in the closet might be salvageable for charity, along with a few pieces of furniture. The rest would simply have to go.

For herself, she couldn't imagine finding anything she would want to keep.

But there, it turned out, she was wrong. On the top shelf of the closet she came upon an old hatbox covered in faded floral paper. It felt unexpectedly heavy.

Slowly, she put it down on the bed and lifted the lid. The box was crammed full of papers. One by one, she began lifting them out. Her breath caught when she realized what they were.

Here was her eighth-grade report card, the one on which her homeroom teacher had written: "Exceptional student, great potential." Here was a drawing she must have done in—what?—second grade, maybe third. Here was a French test she'd aced, a chemistry final she'd gotten a hundred percent on, another drawing, and more and more dating from the time she'd been a toddler all the way to the final weeks she'd spent in her mother's home.

And beyond. For here, too, were newspaper clippings about her books, reviews and copies of the bestseller lists on which she'd appeared. All carefully cut out, none of the edges jagged, and laid meticulously away.

Nickie's eyes burned. Her throat was tight. It hadn't even occurred to her that her mother had kept anything to do with her. Patty had simply never seemed to care.

Yet she had, secretly and alone, she had hidden away what amounted to a record of Nickie's life—and of her success.

It made no sense.

It made perfect sense.

The contradiction overwhelmed her. Holding the faded papers in her hands, she sat on the edge of the bed and stared at the curtains billowing in the breeze.

She had thought to finish this job as quickly as she could and be gone. But now everything seemed far more complicated than she'd expected.

Suddenly she wanted to go slowly through her mother's house, to find out what other surprises it might harbor.

And she wanted to look more closely at the place where she had grown up, the place she had fled from so precipitously.

The place where the waves still pounded against the cliffs and a hazel-eyed man still dwelled.

Chapter 6

Barely had Nickie returned to the Gull's Rest and indicated her intention to stay on for a while than Donna was nodding her head.

"Well, of course, dear, why wouldn't you stay? This is your home, after all, and it's been so very long since you had a chance to visit."

Shrewdly she added, "Even so, you must have noticed that some things don't change."

Nickie sighed, knowing full well what Donna meant. The living room curtain hadn't been fluttering last night for nothing.

Briefly she considered what the reaction would be should she admit that she still found Conor intensely attractive and was probably making the mistake of her life by staying anywhere within his reach.

Of course, wild horses couldn't have compelled her to say any such thing. Her feelings were intensely private and she froze any attempt to intrude on them.

"I'll be going out again now," she said pointedly to Donna, who had positioned herself to block the doorway.

Confronted directly, she had no choice but to move. Nickie made her escape in good order, but once back outside, she was at loose ends. She could hardly follow her instincts and go looking for Conor, but on the other hand she hated the thought of puttering around aimlessly. It simply went against her grain.

The solution to her problem appeared in an unlikely form. She was still standing near her car, trying to decide what to do, when a large, pearl gray Cadillac purred by. Catching sight of her, Ed Mulloney slammed on the brakes hard enough to make the entire front end of the car shudder.

"Hi, there," he yelled cheerfully. His broad forehead puckered as he saw the keys in her hand. "Not leaving, are you?"

Nickie shook her head. She wasn't sure why, but a moment later she heard herself saying, "No, I was just thinking about going for a drive."

That was all the invitation Ed needed. Stretching across the front seat, he flipped the passenger door open. "Always more fun if you've got company. What do you say?"

She hesitated, still unsure of why she was even considering going with him. He didn't attract her. Even without the whole issue of Conor, Ed Mulloney simply wasn't her type.

But the years had taught her to trust her instincts. For some reason she couldn't quite grasp, she felt drawn to know him better. Before she could think better of it, she dropped the keys in her purse and walked toward the car.

"How about the grand tour?" she suggested as she got in. "I've been away for so long that I've practically forgotten everything."

Mulloney beamed her a smile. He really wasn't an unattractive man. In fact, she knew plenty of women who would be drawn to the florid good looks, the blunt self-confidence and the blatantly visible signs of affluence. Whatever else he was, the contractor wasn't shy about letting people know of his success.

They chatted idly, or mostly Ed did, about this project and that, and the great success he'd had. Before Nickie's patience could give out, they pulled up in front of a condominium development about a mile out of town on the shore.

"Lemme tell you," he said as they got out of the car, "I had a hell of a time with this one." He strode across the ground strewn with fragmented clam shells and thrust a large hand out at the two-story buildings sitting white and peaceful in the autumn sun.

"I ask you, does it look like there's anything wrong with this place? Is it dirty or dangerous? Or does it look like the kind of place hardworking people would just love to come to for a little fun and relaxation?"

"It seems fine," she acknowledged as she glanced around. The development wasn't especially large, only a half-dozen buildings grouped around a central courtyard that contained a pool and clubhouse. Some effort had been made at landscaping and the buildings themselves were freshly painted, giving the whole a pleasant, inoffensive air.

"I almost ended up not being able to build it," Ed said with disgust. "All because that friend of yours, Mr. Save-the-Whales McDonnell, got the idea that we'd be chasing away some friggin' birds. Excuse my language, but I just can't understand anybody who puts animals ahead of people. That's the kind of thinking that really gets my goat."

Not to mention threatens your profits, Nickie thought. She wasn't totally unsympathetic to Ed but his slighting reference to Conor had suddenly and painfully alerted her to the reason for her accepting the contractor's company.

The previous day, when they'd met at the Clamshell Café, she had stored away the distinct impression that Ed Mulloney was more dangerous than others might think. It wasn't that she was overly suspicious, on the contrary, she tended to take people at face value. But because of that, she saw Ed clearly and directly, with no evasion. Added to that was her heightened sensitivity to anything involving Conor. She looked, she saw, and she came away worried.

How many times had the two men locked heads before? She knew about Conor's refusal to sell Mulloney the property, and now there was this business

about the condo development. Had there been other
incidents as well?

It didn't take long to learn the answer. All Ed
needed was the slightest hint and he was off and running.

"Ever since he came back here, it's been one thing
after another," he complained when they were once
again in the car. "Every project I come up with, he's
got some complaint against. And it's not just me, he's
doing it to all the developers. Lemme tell you, we're all
getting plenty P.O.'ed."

The litany continued over the lunch Nickie tact-
fully suggested. They went to Norm's, where she ate
surprisingly good curried chicken and lemon sorbet.
Ed's meal was more liquid.

About halfway through it, Nickie realized that he'd
started drinking earlier in the day. The next time he
tried to signal Norm for a refill, the café owner appeared not to notice. Even so, by the time they were
finished, Nickie was genuinely worried about getting
back in the car with him.

Norm had idled over to the door, where he seemed
to be staring off into space. As Ed fumbled for his
keys, Norm murmured, "That sure is some fine car
you've got, Mr. Mulloney. What do you say, Miss
Chandler, you ever drive anything like that?"

Nickie shot Norm a sharp glance, saw nothing but
bland cheerfulness, and made a mental note to take a
closer look at him sometime. In the meanwhile, she
said, "As a matter of fact I never have, but I'd sure
love to give it a try."

Very rarely did Nickie make any attempt to use her beauty to achieve her objectives. The very thought made her feel intensely awkward. But this time she was willing to make an exception.

The smile she flashed Mulloney was the kind heroines in her books sometimes used, seeming to promise far more than they knew. It worked.

He did a double-take, grinned, and handed over the keys. "Sure, honey, enjoy yourself."

Ed slumped in the passenger seat as Nickie drove at a sedate pace, trying to disguise the fact that she really wasn't sure where she should go. Ed's condition ruled out any more sight-seeing. She would have liked to return to Gull's Rest and pick up her own car, but that left the problem of what to do with him. At last, inspiration struck.

"You know," she said, "I'm thinking about writing a book that has a builder as the hero, but I'm having problems with the setting. Would you mind if I took a look at your offices?"

Big surprise, he didn't. The headquarters of Mulloney Development were toward the center of the island, not far from the airport. In addition to the main office, there were several outbuildings.

"We've got a complete operation right here in one location," Ed said proudly. Alcohol made him even more talkative. "See there, the new warehouse holds enough lumber to put up a three-story building. Concrete and asphalt are kept over that way, and there—" he added as he pointed to a small shed on the distant edge of the property "—there's my personal favorite, the explosive depot. Got enough nitro in there to blow a crater the size of a football field.''

Nickie didn't know whether to believe him or not. The thought was appalling yet it was also possible. "It doesn't make you nervous working near something like that?" she asked carefully.

"'Course not. I've handled plenty of nitro in my time. Nothing to be scared of long as you know what you're doing. Come on," he continued, "lemme show you what I got inside here."

The main office had been refurbished recently, down to the new computer system of which Ed was inordinately proud. Even half crocked as he was, he made a show of demonstrating it for her.

"Looka this," he said as he pushed buttons clumsily. "You can get anything you want—plans, specs, eleba—elevations. Does the work of a dozen designers. With this baby behind me, there's no limit to how far I can go."

His smile faded as a look of momentary puzzlement flitted across his face. It took that long for him to remember why, with this baby already behind him, he wasn't expanding at the pace he desired.

"'Course you can't do anything without land," he said. "And every time I go after a piece, I run smack up against *him.*"

There was no need to ask who he meant. Watching him, Nickie thought uneasily that Conor seemed to be almost an obsession with the contractor. It was as though he blamed Conor for all his problems, whether Conor actually had anything to do with them or not.

Once again, the tremor of fear she had felt before whispered through Nickie. Because of her experience with her mother, she had a deeply rooted dread of people who drank too much. She had learned at an early age to cajole and conspire simply to survive. While she wasn't devoid of sympathy, she had a hard core of distrust nothing could erase.

Slowly she looked at Ed. The big, well-dressed man appeared perfectly normal, if somewhat morose. Seated at the computer console, it was impossible to even tell that he'd been drinking. When he got up, the effect was more evident, but even so he hardly appeared dangerous.

Nonetheless, she was overcome by a sudden need to leave. As a child, she had dreamed of escape. Now that she was a grown woman, there was nothing to stop her from doing so.

"Thanks for the tour," she said as she moved toward the door. "I don't want to keep you any longer."

He looked surprised. "Hey, you don't have to go. There's plenty more to see."

She shook her head, smiling pleasantly but firmly. "You've got work to do and I promised myself a nice long walk this afternoon. But thanks all the same. Another time."

Oblivious to how anxious she was to be gone, he was about to persist when one of his employees thankfully appeared, bearing news of some problem that required immediate attention. Grumbling, Ed went off, complaining loudly that nobody could do anything without him and what did he pay them all for anyway?

Once outside, Nickie took a deep, relieved breath. She supposed that she'd overreacted a little but couldn't regret it. Ed Mulloney scared her, plain and simple. Not for herself, there was nothing he could do to her. It was Conor she was thinking of as she walked slowly along the road.

It led away from the main highway toward the beach. She paused for a few minutes, gazing out across the sea and sand. Gradually a sense of peacefulness stole over her, replacing the anxiety she had been feeling.

She strolled along, the toes of her boots sinking into the sand and the cool air lifting the ends of her hair. As a child, she had loved the beach in all seasons. But later she had been far too busy working to enjoy it.

Until that night with Conor...

She stopped abruptly and looked around her. A flush crept over her cheeks that had nothing to do with the wind. She couldn't believe what she had done. How could she have managed to find her way back to the exact spot where she and Conor had first made love?

Yet there it was, no mistake. Where the cliffs rose above the beach, immense boulders were tossed about, creating a sheltered nest of golden sand in between them.

She had sat there on one of the rocks, her legs bare and tan, her eyes filled with wonder, careless of the world . . . the future . . . everything.

He had reached up to her, his powerful arms open, beckoning, and she had gone without a second thought, without regrets, gone to the pleasure and the passion her life had been so bereft of until that moment.

Somewhere deep in her soul she'd realized that he longed for love as much as she did, had been denied it in his own way as much as she had been. It was left to the two of them, hidden in the depths of the rock forest, to find that love together.

Magical. There was no other word for what they had shared. Except perhaps, hopeless.

"I don't understand," he'd said that last day when she'd told him she was leaving. "Why are you doing this?"

There was no way to explain to him that the passion he had unleashed in her was as terrifying as it was exalting. Her life was built on rigid self-control. It kept her going through the darkest times, kept her striving for a better future. A future of her own making. A future where she—who had always felt helpless in the face of her mother's sickness—would feel helpless no more.

He was another kind of helplessness, a terrible vulnerability that made her feel lost and afraid. It wasn't his fault, he wasn't to blame. It was simply the way things were.

The way she was.

"Be my wife," he had said in a last-ditch effort to keep her.

How could she refuse? He was young, gloriously handsome, magnificently sensual and wealthy to boot. What woman in her right mind could possibly turn him down?

And yet…if she agreed, where would that leave her? An appendage on Conor's arm, one who would never truly fit into his world. His parents would undoubtedly despise her, his friends wouldn't know what to make of her, and as for herself—she was terrified that she would end up feeling more alone than she had all her life.

"The scholarship—" she said, fumbling. "I'm going to college next month." Through dint of tireless effort, she had managed to gain a scholarship that would pay half her expenses at a small Midwestern university. For the rest, she would have to rely on her savings and the jobs she planned to get.

"Come to Boston with me," he said easily. "There are plenty of schools there."

But not plenty that would give her a scholarship. Of that she was quite sure. She was good, but not good enough to attract the interest of a Harvard or an M.I.T. type school.

And Conor's money was tied up in a trust fund from his grandmother that wouldn't come due before his twenty-fifth birthday. So long as he more or less behaved himself and did as his parents wanted, they gave him an absurdly generous allowance. But the day

he announced his engagement to Nickie, she had no
doubt the largess would end.

"You just don't know, do you?" she said sadly.
"Without money, the world can be a horrible place.
You've never had to deal with that, but I have."

He would come to hate her, as she believed deep
down inside that her mother already did. She would be
a terrible burden around his neck, robbing him of the
life he wanted.

Before she let that happen, she would walk away
cold and never look back.

"I have to make it on my own," she said, ignoring
the pain twisting inside her. "I simply have to. For me,
there is no alternative."

He had understood then, if only because he'd had
no choice. The summer was ending. Already the sea-
sonal birds were heading south. It was a time for re-
treating.

"Which is exactly what I did," she murmured to
herself. For the first time, she forced herself to con-
front the truth of what had made her reject Conor.

What had terrified her, above all else, was the need
to give herself to another person, not for a brief, pas-
sion-inspired moment, but forever. To do that, she
would have had to drop the defenses woven throughout her childhood, truly open her heart and soul to
another's touch.

And that, she simply had not been able to do. Not
when she was eighteen. And not now. The wounds still
ran too deep.

But they might be healed. For the first time, she felt genuinely hopeful that she could put the past behind her.

The question was, could Conor?

Chapter 7

Conor finished collecting the last of the day's water samples and stood up slowly. He stared at the clear plastic container without really seeing it. In his mind's eye, he was already anticipating what he would find when he looked at the sample under the microscope in his cabin.

Yesterday, he hadn't liked what he'd seen. He had the distinct feeling that he would like it even less today. The sample would have to be sent on for further tests, of course, but years of experience had taught him what the likely outcome would be.

A certain amount of pollution was inevitable, but what he was seeing now went well beyond any accepted limits. Moreover, the particular type of pollution—chemical solvents that would not easily decompose in water—were especially dangerous to marine life and everything else that came in contact with them. Including the people unfortunate enough to eat contaminated seafood.

Stupid bastards, he thought as he rose and put the sample container in his backpack. No matter how hard he tried, he would never understand such short-sightedness.

The same people who dumped dangerous wastes without thought to where they would end up had to live in the world themselves. They had families who would suffer the consequences along with everyone else. Did they ever think of that or did the money wash out every trace of conscience?

He found the Jeep where he had parked it at the end of the dirt road and got in behind the wheel. The back of his neck hurt. He rubbed it reflexively as he glanced at the clock on the dashboard. It was later than he'd thought. No wonder he was hungry.

He hadn't felt like eating when he woke up, drawn from restless sleep with a feeling of depression that was totally unlike him. Not even when his father's crimes became known and he was left to carry the burden of them alone had Conor felt such grimness.

Only once before in his life had he experienced the dark, smothering sense that threatened him now. When Nickie had left, the light had seemed to go out of the world.

It had been a struggle to fight his way through and put his life back in order. But he'd been younger then and buoyed up by the resilience of anger. Now he wasn't sure what he was going to do.

Work, as always, proved an invaluable release. He plunged into it with all the tenacious strength of his character. Without boasting, he knew that native intelligence and a capacity for endless effort were rapidly making him one of the top men in his field. Unlike many others, he had his choice of research grants and there were any number of university positions waiting for him the moment he decided to leave full-time fieldwork.

As he shifted gears, he glanced around at the sun-dappled pine forest. The deep breath he took filled his lungs with clean, sweet air. All around him, he could hear the muted rustle of small creatures preparing for their winter sleep. It was all comfortingly familiar yet eternally new.

He was glad he'd come back to the island, although at the time he'd had some doubts. Now he was sure this was where he belonged. The land and sea he fought to protect had taken the place of the family he didn't have. He nurtured them as he would a wife and children.

And yet there were times when his work wasn't enough. Seeing Nickie again had made him aware of the vacuum in his life.

He shook his head ruefully. It was absurd that he had never been able to forget the girl he had loved ten years before. He should have moved on. And he had tried, but always there was a sense of falseness. His innately honest nature would not allow him to pretend something that wasn't true.

He broke off his thoughts to concentrate on driving. The dirt road was badly rutted. At the moment, he couldn't afford an expensive repair bill. What extra money he had was drained away by the house in town.

Merely keeping it in semi-decent shape was costing him a bundle and that would only increase once the winter set in. Yet no matter what the hardship, he couldn't bring himself to sell to Ed Mulloney or anyone like him.

The dirt road ended at last. He picked up speed and was doing about fifty when he spotted the figure up ahead. She was dressed in jeans and a loose sweater, the same as a hundred other girls, but there was no mistaking Nickie. The sunlight dancing in her hair, the thoroughbred grace of her stride, the special tilt of her head were all achingly familiar.

"Want a lift?" he asked as he drew up beside her.

She'd stopped at the sound of the motor and was looking at him with an expression he couldn't read. After a moment a tentative smile lifted the corners of her mouth.

"Sure, why not?"

He wanted to ask what she was doing this far out, but he sensed a certain reticence about her that kept his curiosity in check.

"Beautiful day," she said as she settled back in the seat. Her features looked composed, almost peaceful, without the tension he had felt in her before.

"Nothing beats autumn here," he said as he pressed down on the gas again. "The people who leave at Labor Day don't know what they miss."

"Maybe it's just as well," Nickie mused. "It's nice to have the place to ourselves."

It didn't escape Conor that she was instinctively including herself among the natives who took a possessive pride in the island and only grudgingly tolerated the visitors whose money they depended on. Yet surely she was planning to leave soon...wasn't she? It couldn't take all that long to clean out Patty Chandler's small cottage.

She was staring out the window, watching the pine forest flow by. Abruptly she said, "I saw Ed Mulloney again."

Conor stiffened. His instant reaction was intense and revealing. A wave of anger rose up in him. With an almost visible effort, he struggled to restrain it. "What did he have to say?"

"Mostly he talked about you and how much trouble you're giving him."

Conor laughed caustically. "He doesn't know what trouble really is. But then this is a guy who thinks AstroTurf and plastic flowers are the highest expression of good taste."

"Maybe so, but he's smart enough to give people what they want. Those condos he built aren't bad."

"They're too close to fragile wetlands, the ground under them is shifting and the water supply is iffy. I wouldn't call that good."

"He says you almost stopped the development."

"Unfortunately, I came in too late. But people are wising up. It's only going to get tougher for Mulloney and others like him."

"What do you suppose he'll do about that?" she asked.

Conor shrugged. "Who knows? If he's got any sense at all, he'll take his money and move on."

Perhaps, but Nickie doubted that. For all his apparent weaknesses, the contractor had a tenacity that worried her. Moreover, his anger against Conor seemed to have taken on a very personal tone that went far beyond the usual business differences.

She almost said as much but thought better of it. Conor wouldn't believe her. She wasn't absolutely sure she should, either.

She'd had a disturbing encounter with the man that had made her think painfully about her mother. There was nothing new about that. Whenever she saw somebody who drank too much, she thought of Patty.

Nickie had paid the bills at the nursing home, kept in touch, had even visited her mother from time to time. But she had never been able to shake the feeling that the woman who had given birth to her was somebody she would never know, never be able to understand.

The gulf between them was simply too wide. It had left her with an iron-clad determination to depend on no one except herself.

Until she'd opened the faded hatbox and discovered that perhaps they hadn't been so far apart, after all.

Belatedly, she became aware of Conor's silence. She had wandered off into her own thoughts so completely that he might well have considered her rude. But when she attempted to apologize, he waved it off.

"I do the same thing myself. We're both old enough to have things in our lives that we're still trying to come to terms with."

Softly, not wanting to intrude too much, she said, "I really am sorry about your father, Conor. It must have come as a tremendous shock."

To her surprise, he shook his head. "Not really. Don't get me wrong, there were things I respected about Dad. But I think I always knew that he cared more for appearances than reality. It was extremely important to him that he be seen to live well, even when that meant stealing money from the bank to do it."

"Still, he must have had doubts about what he was doing."

"You mean because he had a heart attack when he was found out? Maybe so. He probably couldn't have tolerated prison and that was definitely where he was headed. His doctors told me that he'd had a good chance of pulling through if he'd just tried, but he gave up."

As her mother had done, Nickie thought, and Conor's mother, too, for that matter. Didi preferred a life of protected leisure with another man to dealing with the tragedy that had overtaken her husband. Conor might be forgiven if he thought people weren't too reliable.

"Look," he said suddenly, "if it's all the same to you, I'd like to drop some stuff off before I drive you back."

Conor's cabin was small and rustic, nestled up against a finger of water that wrapped its way around a small, shell-strewn beach. Pine trees stood sentinel all around, their fallen needles forming a softly scented blanket that covered the ground.

"How beautiful," Nickie murmured. It was no exaggeration. The McDonnells' shining house on the hill might be grand and elegant, but this place had a natural grandeur nothing could surpass.

"I like it," Conor said matter-of-factly. He removed his backpack from the rear of the Jeep and stood aside to let her precede him up the path to the front door. Unusually for the island, it was locked.

"I keep a fair amount of equipment on hand," he explained as he unlocked the door and opened it. "No sense tempting fate."

Certainly not, but Nickie had the feeling that there was another, unstated reason for his concern with security. He had fumbled slightly with the key as though he wasn't in the habit of using it despite the impression he gave. Yet the equipment he mentioned looked as though it had been in place for some time.

A microscope and centrifuge occupied one side of a low worktable that was placed against the far wall. On the other side was a sophisticated computer setup, far more advanced than the one Ed had so proudly displayed. It, in turn, was linked to a telephone console and fax machine.

"It looks as though you've got everything you could possibly need," Nickie said.

Besides the technical equipment, the cabin was simply but comfortably furnished. An overstuffed couch sat in front of the fireplace. Low tables held a selection of books and magazines, most of them looking dog-eared.

In the far corner, next to the back door, narrow stairs led to the loft bedroom. A compact kitchen and bath completed the interior.

Nickie looked around with unfeigned interest. No attempt had been made to make the decor particularly masculine yet she felt that if she had been dropped down here without explanation, she would have intuitively thought of Conor. The tasteful prints on the walls, the books strewn around, the casual neatness all carried the imprint of his personality.

"I'm starving," Conor said. "How about joining me?"

Belatedly, she realized how hungry she was and nodded. "Can I help?"

He agreed and they went together into the small kitchen. Nickie perched on a stool beside the counter, tearing up lettuce for salad while Conor made omelets.

Glancing at him out of the corner of her eye, she could see that he was obviously experienced at fending for himself. Moreover, he seemed to enjoy cooking. Almost to herself, she laughed.

"What's funny?" he asked.

"I was just remembering a job I had in college working as a short-order cook. What a disaster that was. I barely lasted a week. It was right about then that I decided I'd better get serious about writing. It was the only thing I had a real shot at doing."

"So something good came out of it after all," Conor said as he took the salad bowl from her.

His expression was perfectly pleasant, but she had the sense that he was referring to more than her short stint at the diner. Something good had come out of her leaving him. She had fulfilled her dream of being successful and respected.

But it no longer seemed enough.

"Grab a couple of glasses, will you?" Conor asked.

She did as he said and caught up with him as he was setting the food out on a low coffee table across from the fireplace.

"I keep meaning to get something else to eat on," he said, "but I've never gotten around to it. When it's usually just me, there doesn't seem much point."

Usually—not always. Nickie reflected on that as she took her seat. She didn't suppose there were too many women who would object to dining in such surroundings with Conor. On the contrary, she was only surprised that one of them hadn't already taken up residence.

"This is good," she said after she'd taken a bite of the omelet. He'd seasoned it with a handful of herbs that still tasted fresh from the garden.

They ate in silence for a few minutes before she became aware of Conor watching her. There was noth-

ing covert about it. He simply looked at her straight
out, his hazel eyes alight with thoughts she couldn't
read.

Suddenly self-conscious, she raised a hand to touch
her hair, a nervous gesture he recognized.

"What?" she murmured.

He smiled ruefully. "Sorry, I was just thinking how
odd all this is. If anybody had told me a few days ago
that the two of us would be sitting here having dinner, I'd have thought it was crazy."

"Why?" she asked. "We're both adults. Surely
there's no reason why we can't be friends."

He didn't answer at once. Instead he merely sat back
and studied her. Outside, the light was beginning to
fade. In the golden twilight streaming through the
windows, his skin looked burnished, his features hard
and unrelenting. In his face, only his eyes were alive.

She fastened on them, waiting, hardly breathing,
until he said, "Yes, Nickie, there is a reason and we
both know what it is." Gently, he drew her to him.

Chapter 8

His mouth was cool and inviting. He touched her lips gently, demanding nothing, giving her time to come to him.

At first, she thought that she wouldn't be able to. It had been so long and she had fought so hard to repress the feelings that were now surging forward, demanding release.

She was afraid, yet this was Conor, who had never hurt her, who had only loved her and wanted to share his life with her.

He was so gentle. Had the years done that to him or was it mere experience? Ten years before he had been a young man filled with hungry urgency. He hadn't hurt her, not at all, but neither had he been so achingly tender.

Unlike now. Slowly, almost imperceptibly, Nickie began to relax. Her lips parted on a soft sigh of pleasure. Instinctively she moved closer.

Conor's powerful arms closed around her, as though he was still afraid that she might pull back. He wanted to do nothing to frighten or displease her.

Slowly, reluctantly, he had come to terms with the fact that he was still intensely drawn to her. Exactly how such a thing was possible, he didn't know, but he had seen enough of nature to know that it seemed to work toward some essential harmony beyond the ability of mere humans to comprehend.

Not that it was harmony he was feeling now as her full, high breasts brushed against his chest. Through the layers of their clothes, he was achingly conscious of her body, slender but curved, soft as only a woman's could be, strong yet vulnerable.

He was going to lose his mind if he couldn't have more of her, couldn't rid himself of the terrible, driving need that had seized him. Half angry, remembering the pain she had inflicted all those years before, he clasped the back of her head in his hand and held her still for him.

The hot thrust of his tongue took Nickie by surprise, but with it came a bolt of pleasure so intense as to banish all hesitancy. She met his caresses with her own, tasting and savoring him until she felt as though her body was being consumed by fire.

Her hands shook as she found the buttons of his shirt and began to undo them. His chest was broad, tautly muscled and covered with a fine dusting of dark brown hair. Their mouths clung as she touched him, loving the rippling strength, the iron-hard contours, the sheer, sensual feel of him.

"Sweet heaven, Nickie," he muttered under his breath. "Don't stop."

She truly didn't think that she would have been able to under any circumstances. Boldness she had never known before had seized her. She tore her lips from his and ran her tongue down the hard line of his throat to his collarbone and below.

His skin was hot and slightly salty. They had slipped off the couch onto the thickly carpeted floor. His body cradled hers protectively. She felt his hands at her waist, pulling up the heavy turtleneck sweater, and moved slightly to make it easier for him.

Cool air touched her skin but she was hardly aware of it. All she could see was his face, suffused with passion as he looked at her.

"Beautiful," he said huskily as he cupped her breasts in his big, hard hands. Through the lacy fabric of her bra, he rubbed her nipples gently. Nickie moaned and bit her lower lip. Deep within, she could feel her muscles clenching.

The bra had a front closing. He smiled faintly as he opened it and slid the straps from her shoulders. She could see the smoldering hunger in his eyes, feel the overwhelming tenseness of his body, but none of that frightened her. On the contrary, she gloried in his touch and in the knowledge that she could, in turn, bring him to transcendent pleasure.

Their clothes fell away assisted by urgent tugs and murmurs of encouragement. He was so magnificently beautiful that her breath caught in her throat when she saw him at last.

The broad sweep of his shoulders and chest all but blocked out the fading light. In the shadows, her gaze ran over the flat expanse of his abdomen, his narrow hips, the steely thighs and the burgeoning manhood lying between them.

Unconsciously, her lips parted. He was very large and it had been so long. . . .

As though he sensed her unease, Conor ran his hands slowly down the length of her. She shivered responsively, instinctively moving closer, wanting only what he could give.

"Easy," he murmured, "there's no rush."

He spoke more confidently than he felt. The mounting pressure of his loins was explosive. He had been too long without a woman, preferring celibacy to relationships that were empty and meaningless. He didn't regret that now, except in so far as it might make him too hasty with Nickie.

For all his contradictory feelings about this woman, he suddenly couldn't bear the thought of hurting her. She sensed it and drew closer. Against her smooth, scented skin, he murmured, "I didn't want it to be like this. It should be perfect."

"It is," she said. Her full mouth, swollen from his kisses, curved in a smile. Her blue-green eyes were slumberous, the lids heavy with passion. So very long . . .

Her slender hand slipped between them, cool fingers finding and caressing him. He gasped as the last rigid bond on his control snapped.

Even then he was careful, waiting until he was certain of her readiness before moving within her. The hard, smooth crest of his manhood teased her soft, moist flesh.

She sobbed his name as her hips arched. Against the smooth inner flesh of her thighs, she felt the hair-roughened strength of his. She was open, wanting, unbearably aroused. If he waited a moment longer...

He did not, thrusting into her with a strength and passion that robbed her of all breath. For an instant, her eyes fluttered shut and she heard a great whirring as if a door had opened on eternity itself. Then the world righted and she was safe in Conor's arms, their bodies intimately joined.

His gaze held hers as he began to move with devastating skill. "Look at me, Nickie," he commanded hoarsely. "I want you to know who this is, to remember it forever."

Because he expected her to leave again. Dimly she realized that and wanted to protest. How could anything so magnificent ever end? Surely it would go on forever, like the sun that was rushing down to greet them, hurtling them into a realm neither had ever touched before.

Ten years ago their lovemaking had been beautiful and fulfilling. But this went beyond anything they had known then. They were older, wiser, more capable of the selfless giving that transformed desire into something vastly deeper.

Lying beneath him, holding him within her, Nickie felt the first deep tremors of approaching completion. Part of her wanted to delay it, to hold off as long as she could. But the sheer force of the moment was too great.

Her head fell back, pillowed on her honey-spun hair. Her eyes met Conor's, seeing in them ruthless power and will. Before she could consider that too closely, release overcame her and she knew nothing more.

Chapter 9

Much later, they made their way up the narrow staircase and fell into the wide, welcoming bed. There they made love again, more slowly this time. Afterward, they slept.

It was dawn when Nickie awoke again. She lay for a moment, staring up at the rough-hewn ceiling uncomprehendingly. This wasn't her apartment, nor was it the room at Gull's Rest.

Memory returned slowly. She sat up, holding the sheet to her breasts, and stared at the man asleep beside her. Awake he was formidable, filled with male strength and determination. Sleep gentled him somewhat, smoothing the lines from his face and bestowing haunting echoes of the boy he had once been.

She leaned forward, watching the play of light and shadow over his burnished skin. A night's growth of beard roughened the smooth line of his jaw. His lips were slightly parted, his breathing slow and even.

Slowly she bent her head and touched her mouth to his. There was no response. She grew bolder, touching him with the tip of her tongue.

Still nothing. Caught between amusement and chagrin, she slid her hand down and drew the sheet from his chest and hips. Her eyes followed, widening.

"Oh..."

"Surprise," he murmured at the same instant that his arms closed around her.

"You're awake," she said, pressing her hands against his chest in halfhearted resistance.

The grin he shot her, coupled with the lock of chestnut hair falling over his forehead, gave him a roguish look. A tremor of anticipation rippled through her. The many facets of lovemaking were still so new to her, she longed to experience them all.

She said nothing, but the unfeigned yearning in her eyes made Conor's throat tighten. She was filled with so many contrasts, at once innocent and sophisticated, indomitable yet fragile. He could spend a lifetime loving her and still find more mysteries to be solved.

A lifetime. Abruptly he stiffened. He was a damned fool to be thinking in such terms. Nickie had made it crystal clear how she felt about the island and about him. Both might be enjoyable for a short time but her real life lay elsewhere.

He couldn't even blame her for it. She had the same right as everyone else to choose her own destiny. He could only wish that his wasn't to desire her so senselessly.

In his arms, warm against his body, she nonetheless felt his withdrawal. "Conor...?" she murmured.

His eyes focused on hers but only for an instant did she catch a glimpse of what he was thinking. A shutter seemed to slip into place, closing him off from her.

"It's getting late," he said as he gently but firmly disentangled her arms and stepped from the bed. In the full light of day, he was magnificent. Her breath caught in her throat as she looked at him.

Suddenly aware of her own nakedness, Nickie flushed. She didn't understand what had gone wrong, but obviously something had. Conor looked completely absorbed in his own thoughts as he dressed. She might not even have existed.

Abruptly she was angry. He had no right to treat her this way, not under any circumstances, but most especially not after what they had shared.

"I'll make some coffee," he said quietly after he was dressed.

She ignored him. The moment he disappeared down the stairs, she rose and threw on her clothes. Her throat was very tight and her eyes burned.

She had to struggle against the need to cry, but was damned if she'd do it here in this place. Instead she fiercely focused her attention on the simple task of getting away.

"No thanks," she said curtly when she came downstairs to find he had already poured a cup for her. She wished desperately that she had her car with her and could simply get in it and escape, but she was miles from anywhere and much as she hated it, dependent on him.

"If you wouldn't mind driving me to the main road," she said, not looking at him, "I can get a lift from there."

His face darkened, the eyes suddenly thunderous. "What are you talking about? You're not hitching anywhere."

"It's perfectly safe," she said stubbornly, "now that the tourists are gone." Bluntly she added, "Besides, if you drive me back to Gull's Rest, Donna will be sure to see and I really don't need her spreading gossip about us that is completely unfounded."

His eyebrows rose, accentuating the hardness of his gaze. "Completely?" he repeated, the challenge clear in his tone.

Coldly, she turned away from him. She needed no reminders of what had passed between them, or of how he had followed it by withdrawing from her. Pride demanded that she give him no hint of the torment she was suffering.

What a fool she had been to believe that the past could be recaptured. They were both different people now, with different agendas. It was inevitable that they would go their separate ways.

"If you don't mind," she said pointedly, gesturing toward the door.

Conor muttered under his breath and slammed his coffee mug down. He yanked open the door and stood aside. As she brushed past him, their bodies touched, sending a shock through them both.

Scrupulously, Nickie kept her eyes blank as she climbed into the Jeep. Conor started it with an angry jerk but instantly eased off, his customary control reasserting itself. Despite the waves of tension she felt coming from him, he drove sensibly.

They reached the main road but he didn't stop. She glanced at him, wanting to remind him but guessing that his temper was not so stringently controlled as to bear testing just then. Instead she bit her lip and kept silent as he drove her into town, not stopping until they were a block away from the guest house.

As he pulled over to the curb, he glanced at her coldly. "I hope this doesn't offend your sense of propriety too much."

A dozen replies sprang to her mind, all of them nasty. She settled on silence and let herself out of the Jeep before Conor could intervene. Nonetheless, she could not prevent him from getting out, which he immediately did. Deliberately, he blocked her path.

"Nickie," he said, his face softening, "I'm sorry this went wrong. I truly didn't mean to hurt you. It's just that—"

"Forget it," she interrupted. "It's not important."

That was an outright lie since surely nothing had ever been more important to her. But she was not about to admit that to herself, much less to him.

Without giving him the chance to reply, she moved past him and walked steadily away. His gaze burned into a spot immediately between her shoulder blades but she refused to look back, knowing that were she to do so, he would see the tears coursing silently down her pale cheeks.

Chapter 10

By the time she reached Gull's Rest, Nickie had managed to compose herself sufficiently to mask all signs of the emotional turmoil raging inside. This was fortunate since barely had she opened the front door then she came face-to-face with Donna.

The older woman gave her a hard, knowing look that was instantly masked by an expression of concern.

"There you are, dear. I was a little worried when you didn't come in last night. Of course, you have a perfect right to come and go as you please."

"I should hope so," Nickie murmured, unable for the moment to keep up the burden of false courtesy. "Since I'm paying for the privilege. Excuse me," she added, drawing Donna's attention to the fact that she had positioned herself directly in front of the staircase.

The older woman hesitated, torn between avid curiosity and the need to honor the social forms at least outwardly. With obvious reluctance, she stepped aside, but not without a parting shot.

"A word to the wise, dear. It never does to make a fool of yourself twice." With a self-righteous smile, she swept out of the hall and disappeared through the swinging doors to the kitchen.

Nickie's hand trembled on the stair rail. The nerve of that old harridan. How dare she— Her thoughts broke off, shattered by the grim knowledge that Donna was right.

Ten years ago she had been a fool for Conor, loving him with all the fervent strength of her young heart and body. Loving him so much that the very force of her emotions had terrified her and compelled her to flee.

Had she been a fool again to try even briefly to recapture what had once been? Or was there something essential that she was missing, something vital that had escaped her notice?

She shut her eyes for a moment, trying to still the whirling clamor of her mind. To a certain extent she succeeded, but she knew herself well enough to be sure that the effect would not last for long.

Upstairs in her room, she quickly washed, then changed her clothes. With her face freshly made up and her hair twined in a gleaming chignon at the nape of her neck, she felt once more in control.

As much as was possible, she had eradicated all signs of the passionate woman she had been the night before. The face that looked back at her from the mirror was coolly self-possessed and showed no sign of any emotion other than calmness.

Which was exactly as she wished, but not enough. Heading out of the house and to the car, she wryly acknowledged that what she needed was activity and contact with other people to stop her from dwelling too much on her own problems. Off hand she couldn't think of too many people on the island who would make good company for her at that moment. Certainly Donna would not and Ed was out of the question.

She drove aimlessly for a short while until she found herself on the road that ran past the Clamshell Café. From the look of the parking lot in front, the place was empty.

Norm was at the bar, as usual, perched on a stool with a book in his hand and an absent look on his face. He glanced up as Nickie came in.

"Mornin'," he said, "something I can do for you?"

That seemed an odd question to Nickie. Surely most people who walked into a restaurant were in search of food. There was no reason for her to be considered an exception.

"Breakfast?" she suggested tentatively.

Norm appeared to think that over. At length, he nodded. "That sounds like a good idea. Why don't you take a seat and tell me what you want?"

She settled in at a corner table covered with a red-checked cloth and set with a small glass vase that held a fragrant sprig of sea grass. When Norm had filled her coffee cup and taken her order, she looked around slowly.

When she had visited the café with Conor, her attention had been taken up with the conflict between him and Ed. She hadn't had much chance to appreciate her surroundings, but now she did.

The small interior was meticulously clean and plainly furnished, but with many touches—such as the sea grass—that were unaffected and pleasing. Soft rhythm and blues played in the background. A fresh breeze blew in through a partly opened window.

The scent of good, strong coffee lay on the air. Nickie took a sip and felt herself subtly relaxing. She was beginning to think that she had overreacted to Conor's behavior.

Maybe she should have stayed, tried to talk with him instead of running away. But her pride had been so hurt. He had made her feel like poor little Nickie again.

A warm flush stained her cheeks. Norm came over to the table with a platter of blueberry pancakes. He put them down and looked at her.

Without warning, he said, "Tough comin' home again, isn't it?"

Nickie looked up and met his eyes, finding them unexpectedly lively and filled with compassion. Slowly, she said, "Much tougher than I ever imagined."

"You could leave," he pointed out matter-of-factly.

"I plan to. I only came for a few days to..."

"Settle some old business?" There was nothing offensive in his tone. On the contrary, he spoke as though the desire to leave nothing undone in life was the most natural thing in the world.

A moment passed, then another. Slowly Nickie said, "Would you like to sit down?"

They talked for an hour. Norm told her of his wanderings as a young man in the 1960s, how he had bummed his way across America, ending up finally in the Haight-Ashbury section of San Francisco.

"I don't remember much about that part," he said frankly. "I was too far out of it most of the time. I did so many drugs that I think my brain ended up like scrambled eggs. There's a good chance I'd never have made it except I wandered into this shelter one night and the priest who was running the place helped me get straight."

"How did he do that?" Nickie asked, knowing how many people went down that road and never made it back, no matter how hard they tried.

"He made me understand that by taking drugs I was running away from life. He asked me flat out what was so bad about it that I'd want to do that. One morning he took me out to the beach and made me look, really look, at a sunrise. It sounds corny but he got across the idea that the same thing that had made all that beauty had made me and cared about me. I can't tell you exactly why, but it did the trick."

"So you came back here?"

He nodded. "Believe me, it was tough. Everybody here pretty well knew about me, or thought they did, and they didn't exactly roll out the red carpet. But after a while, they kind of lost interest and I was able to get on with things."

"What do you do?" Nickie asked softly. "I mean, besides running the café?"

"I read," Norm said simply. "Fiction, poetry, philosophy, you name it, I read it. And you know something, the priest was right. We really are supposed to be happy. It's just getting to it that confuses people."

Nickie sighed. To her surprise, she had finished her pancakes. She didn't normally eat much for breakfast but today she was glad that she'd made an exception. She took another sip of her coffee as she considered what Norm had said.

All her life, for as long as she could remember, she had presumed that being in control of her own life would make her happy. Except that it hadn't worked out that way. She felt dogged by something that was not yet completed, something that hovered always on the edges of her consciousness, at once tempting and exasperating her.

That, more than anything else, had brought her back to the island. She wanted to settle once and for all the issue of her past so that she could truly begin to create a future.

But that didn't seem to be happening. On the contrary, she seemed to be running once again, trying to escape before she could be hurt, instead of staying and fighting for what she really wanted.

"Thanks, Norm," she said softly as she settled her bill. "Those were about the best pancakes I've ever had."

He nodded gravely. "Any time you're in the mood for more, feel free."

She was smiling as she got back into her car.

Chapter 11

The air was fresher in her mother's house. Blown in through the windows Nickie had left open, it smelled of sea grass and late autumn flowers.

This time she had come prepared. In the kitchen, she set up the coffeepot she'd stopped to buy at the hardware store. While coffee was brewing, she swept the first floor.

When the coffee was done, she filled a mug and with it in hand, stood for a few minutes looking out at the backyard where she had played as a child. For a brief moment she could see herself as she had been then, digging in the sandy soil with a spoon, determinedly dropping in a handful of seeds and covering them with great care, then waiting day after day for something to happen.

The seeds had never sprouted. Perhaps she had buried them too deeply or perhaps the soil simply wasn't good enough. But no matter how hard she'd watched, waiting for the first small sign of life, the ground had remained stubbornly barren.

That small disappointment had hurt out of all proportion. She remembered crying in her bed at night, biting on the twisted sheet so that her mother wouldn't hear, weeping for the lifelessness of it all.

It was right about then that her mother had come home with the rosebush. Someone had given it to her, she said, but Nickie had her doubts. Young as she was, she knew the only people who gave her mother presents were the men who came and went, bearing bottles in brown paper bags or, once, a flashy red dress her mother still had, or thick slabs of steak they cooked for themselves on the old brick barbecue in the yard.

Not rosebushes with root balls that weren't even bound up like the ones at the nursery but that hung loosely, still trailing dark loamy earth.

"You'll have to plant it," her mother had said, dumping the bush down in the center of the kitchen floor. "Just put it out back, okay?"

"How come?" Nickie asked bemusedly.

"Backyard sun's better for roses," her mother said as though everyone knew that.

Steam drifted above the coffee cup. Nickie smiled to herself. It seemed Patty had been right. Remnants of the summer's plumb red roses still twined around the backyard fence. Without anyone to prune them, they'd run wild. The single small bush had become a thicket.

She took a sip of coffee and stepped away from the window. There was work to be done.

By late morning, she had filled several dozen bags with refuse and sorted out pretty much everything that could be saved. Worked at steadily, the job took less time than she'd expected.

It also kept her from thinking about Conor.

But toward noon, with her back aching and her stomach empty, she decided to take a break. The sandwich that had seemed appetizing that morning no longer appealed. She poured another cup of coffee and sat with it at the battered kitchen table, looking around at what she'd accomplished.

The local church would send a truck to pick up what was usable. The rest would be carted away to the dump. Maybe she'd wait until spring to put the cottage on the market or maybe she'd just go ahead and do it now. Either way, the job would be finished. She'd be free to go back to her own life, the one she had worked so very hard to create.

She should be relieved, perhaps even a little happy. Instead, all she felt was a dull ache of regret.

Would it have been any better if she hadn't seen Conor again, hadn't yielded so suddenly and overwhelmingly to the passion she had wanted to believe was long dead?

Would she have rested more easily, then, secure in her illusions?

There was no way to ever know. What was done was done. She could no more blot out the memory of the previous night than she could forget what had happened ten years before. All she could do was try to go on.

With a sigh, she stood up and went over to the kitchen sink to wash out her mug. The rest of the day stretched out in front of her, demanding to be filled. She could go for a walk or a run, catch up on her reading, nap.

Or she could get out her laptop computer and do some more work on her latest book. It was a sensual tale involving a certain renegade English lord and the daring young woman who alternately infuriated and delighted him. Just the kind of story her readers enjoyed most.

There was no doubt about it, she was great at romance so long as it was confined to the pages of a book. When it came to real life, she was a total dud.

Which just went to show that she should stay as far away from it as she could. Being burned once was bad. Twice hurt almost more than she could bear.

She unplugged the coffeemaker and carried it back out to the car. Returning to the house, she went upstairs for a last look around. When she came back down, she was carrying the hatbox. It felt heavy in her arms. She had to set it on a side table while she fished the keys out of her pocket.

She was just closing the door behind her when the Jeep pulled up in front of the house.

Conor got out slowly. His hands were thrust deep in his pockets and his shoulders were slightly hunched. He'd stopped by the Gull's Rest first, only to find her gone. It had taken him a few minutes to figure out where she was likely to be.

He felt like hell. Ever since leaving her near the guest house that morning, he'd been at war with himself. He'd never treated a woman so coldly. It was stupid, rude, and just plain cruel. But he also knew why he'd done it.

The hard fact of the matter was that he didn't react well to fear. And that was exactly what she made him feel—stark, stomach-wrenching fear. The kind he liked to think he was immune to until he found out otherwise.

He'd been doing fine in his life with work he cared about, a routine he was used to, goals he'd carved out for himself. Okay, so he'd been lonely and hadn't seemed able to do anything about that. But lonely wasn't so bad.

It sure as hell beat terrified.

So why was he standing here, staring at her as if he'd been left out in the desert too long?

He cleared his throat and started up the path. She hadn't moved but stood, frozen in place, never taking her gaze off him.

He tried a smile. "I was driving by and thought you might want some help—" Oh, yeah, that sounded great. He was a regular Boy Scout.

With a grimace, he tried again. "Nickie, this morning—" Did he really want to get into that? Her eyes had gone blank. From the look of it, she didn't want to, either.

"How's the cottage going?" he asked.

"Fine." Her voice was soft but wary. It had a quizzical edge, as though she couldn't quite believe he was there and wanted to know why. "I'm almost finished."

His stomach lurched again. The cottage was the only thing keeping her on the island. Wasn't it?

He looked at the key in her hand. "You're quitting for the day?"

She nodded. "There isn't much left to do." She turned slightly to lock the door. As she did, the hatbox began to tip. Conor stepped forward quickly and took it from her.

Nickie looked startled but didn't object. They walked down the path together. He put the box in the back of her car, then straightened.

Cautiously he asked, "If you don't have any plans for this afternoon, how about coming out on the boat?"

Nickie hesitated. She had to be crazy to even consider going with him after what had happened last night. She should be running as fast as she could in the opposite direction. She should—

"Where to?"

"Just around. I have to take some samples farther out."

She took a deep breath and ignored the clamoring voice in the back of her mind. "All right."

They picked up the boat on the inlet near his cabin. Unlike the racing shell she had seen him in earlier, this was a Boston whaler designed to travel fast in rough water.

The last afternoon sun was bright, but the wind was still chilly enough to make Nickie glad of her heavy sweater. The tide was just beginning to turn as they left the shelter of land and headed out toward the open sea.

"The way the currents run around here," Conor said, "anything dumped a mile or so out follows a fairly predictable track toward land. Yesterday, I found some stuff that was dumped recently. I want to see if I can get an idea of where it started from."

"What kind of stuff?" Nickie asked. The subject was safely impersonal but it also interested her. Despite her best resolve, she was curious to know more about him—his work, his motives, his needs. Everything.

Crazy.

"Acetone, formaldehyde, ethanol, a pretty nasty mix."

"Sounds like it." She spoke softly, but inside she was appalled. It wasn't necessary to understand that the chemicals he named were dangerous. How could they possibly have gotten into the water, especially so close to shore where people routinely swam and fished?

"Do you really think they all came from the same source?"

"It's possible. That's what I'm trying to find out."

It was on the tip of her tongue to ask what all this had to do with studying coastal erosion. On the surface, the two didn't seem related. But, then, who was she to say?

Conor was silent as he steered the boat into a dark trough of water where the current ran strongest. Several miles out, he cut the engine and opened a compartment near the wheel to reveal a large metal box.

"Want to help me with this?" he asked.

Nickie nodded. She was still intensely cautious, but having come this far, the best thing she could do was to stay busy. Maybe that way she'd think less about his hard, lithe body, the tingle of excitement she felt simply being near him, the terrible, growing sense that she would never be free of this man no matter how she tried.

"We'll take a range of samples from different depths," Conor was saying. He wasn't looking at her. All his attention seemed focused on the job at hand. "All you have to do is make sure they're labeled and sealed correctly."

That seemed simple enough. They worked together for more than an hour, filling several dozen small vials. The outgoing tide carried them steadily away from their starting point.

Conor straightened, the last of the vials in his hand, and scanned the horizon. Nickie saw the hard, shuttered look in his eyes and instinctively followed his gaze.

Nothing was in sight except a few fishing boats making their way back to port and one or two pleasure craft that hadn't yet been put up for the winter. In the distance, she could make out a thin white rim of beach framed between the gray-blue sea and the pine forest. She thought she could also make out a road cutting through the trees, but she wasn't sure.

"Let's get back," Conor said suddenly. He put the last vial away in the box and started the motor again.

"What is it?"

"Nothing. We're done and it's getting late."

He was lying. She couldn't have said exactly how she knew but she was absolutely sure. He'd seen something—or thought of something—that had made him anxious to leave.

Once again, she scanned the area as far as she could see. Everything appeared normal.

They reached the shore in silence and dropped anchor in the inlet they had left from. Conor carried the samples inside his cabin. Nickie followed. He put the case down on a worktable near the microscope and an array of other equipment.

She stood off to one side, watching him. He seemed to have forgotten her presence, but a moment later, he looked up. Hesitantly, Conor asked, "Can you stay a while longer?"

She wouldn't let herself think that it was her company he wanted. He was simply anxious to get to work but would delay long enough to drive her back if that was what she wanted. Ruefully, she considered what it meant to be outclassed by a test tube. None of her heroines had ever faced that problem.

"Go ahead," she said, gesturing to the worktable.

Still, he hesitated. "You'll be okay?"

She nodded firmly. "Fine. In fact, I'm kind of worn out. I'd just like to relax for a while."

He shot her a quick, appreciative smile and turned back to the table.

Chapter 12

"Dinner's ready," Nickie said. She stuck her head out of the kitchen. Conor was staring into the microscope. He looked up with a start.

"What?"

"Dinner." She smiled cautiously. "I hope you don't mind, but I was getting pretty hungry." That was an understatement. She'd skipped both breakfast and lunch.

He shook his head as though to clear it and glanced toward the window. It was dark outside.

"I'm sorry," he said, half rising. "I had no idea it was so late." The look on his face was genuinely surprised—and apologetic.

"That's all right," she said, and quickly ducked back into the kitchen. Maybe this wasn't such a good idea, after all.

It was just possible that where he was concerned, she had no common sense whatsoever. The thought was frightening, but also undeniably tantalizing.

Conor joined her a moment later. He had run a hand through his thick chestnut hair. She had to resist the impulse to smooth it.

Together they carried dishes to the low table. Conor opened a bottle of wine as she ladled beef stew into bowls. They ate in silence for several minutes.

"I must have been really out of it," he said finally. "I'm sorry."

This was a far cry from the cold, distant man of the morning. She couldn't begin to explain the change in him, but she was glad of it all the same.

"I like to cook," she said, "even though I don't do it very often."

They fell silent again. Most of the stew was gone before she asked, "Did you find anything?"

Conor grimaced. "Too much." He was tempted to tell her more but the subject was ugly and even potentially dangerous. His stronger instinct was to shield her from it.

Besides, the rapport between them was too precious to interrupt. His deep regret for what had happened that morning was coupled with memories of the pleasure they had shared.

"Nickie," he said gently as he reached out a hand and lightly touched the curve of her cheek. To his relief, she didn't pull away, although she did stiffen and look at him with sudden wariness.

"Don't," he said when he saw her lower lip tremble.

A low sigh escaped her. "Oh, Conor," she murmured, "nothing's the way I'm used to."

He couldn't have put it better himself and he was immensely relieved to discover that she felt the same way. That, at least, was a beginning.

"It's all right," he murmured, his arm slipping around her waist. Gently, he drew her to him. His touch was no more than comforting—at first.

Ever since that morning, she had been living on the keen edge of unfulfilled desire. Her breasts were uncomfortably full, the nipples so sensitive that the thin lace of her bra was a discomfort.

She ached for him so much that the sensation terrified her. Blindly, she reached out, stroking the broad expanse of his shoulders and chest. Beneath her touch, he trembled.

"Sweet heaven," he murmured, "what you do to me."

Triumph eased her fear. She smiled and let her head fall back, exposing the smooth white line of her throat. His mouth was hot, demanding, the stroke of his tongue a ripple of fire. She groaned and clasped him more closely, willing herself to be part of him, to dissolve all the barriers, to be truly and completely one.

Yesterday, he had been infinitely gentle. Now he was less so. The need was simply too great and added to it was the sense of time passing, of a moment that would vanish, never to be seized again.

Her sweater came off with the merest rustle and was tossed aside. The rug was warm and soft beneath her. His hands found the waistband of her jeans, tugging them open.

There was no time...only urgent, incandescent passion. His shirt hung open, revealing his bare, smooth chest rippling with muscle. His skin was so warm... She arched against him, her fingers digging into his shoulders.

She heard the rasp of his zipper dimly. No time...hunger, raging beyond control, taking them to the verge of madness and beyond.

"Please," she gasped, reaching down to find him. He was long and hard, leaping hot in her hand. In her.

Their coming together was explosive. Barely had he entered her than she cried out and he felt the first rippling contractions drawing him farther.

He closed his eyes fiercely, struggling to hold on, but the passion was too great. A thick groan escaped him as he plunged into her again and again, until he was lost.

Conor awoke to darkness and the sensation of cold. He lay for a moment, unmoving, trying to recall where he was. His mind was a whirling mist of sensations that only grudgingly sorted themselves out.

Nickie. Slowly he propped himself up on his elbows and looked down at her. She was deeply asleep, lying in the tumult of their discarded clothes. Her face had the paleness of exhaustion and her mouth looked faintly bruised.

Hardly surprising, he thought candidly. Once had not been enough for either of them. They had seemed driven to devour each other. Again and again, they had loved until sleep caught them unawares and carried them off still close within each other's arms.

Reluctantly he moved away. She murmured uneasily and shivered in his absence. Gathering her to him again, he rose and carried her up the stairs to the loft.

Placing her in the bed, he covered her warmly. She snuggled down contentedly, lying on her side with her hands folded under her chin.

He could easily have remained where he was, watching her as she slept, but for the the faint glimmer of moonlight striking the floor and the quicksilver unease moving through him.

For a man who prided himself on self-control, he was remarkably lacking in it where she was concerned. With this second night together, he was more vulnerable to her than ever. Yet she would leave, go back to her life, and he would—what?

Forget her, go on to another woman, tell himself none of it mattered? He'd tried all that ten years before. It hadn't worked then and he had no real reason to believe it would work now.

Like it or not, the more passion they shared, the more time and thought, the more laughter and intimacy, the more pain he could realistically anticipate.

Sleep vanished down the dark meanderings of his thoughts. Dressed in khakis and a roughly woven sweater, he let himself out of the cabin. Night swirled around him.

He felt a sudden, piercing sense of need to share it with Nickie but pushed that firmly aside. He had been alone for a long time. He would be alone again. It was better to remind himself of that.

A short way from the cabin, waves pounded against the beach. The wind blew through the ancient pine trees and around the tangled branches of blackberry bushes shorn of their summer fruit.

With no immediate sense of where he was going, Conor began walking. Sand twisters danced along the road, vanishing as quickly as they appeared. He continued on for a quarter hour, perhaps slightly more, and saw no one.

In the summer there would still have been a few cars out, carrying late party-goers back to their boats or cottages. The island police would still be patrolling. A few wakeful visitors might even be out for a stroll.

But not now. Nothing stirred along the shore road. He walked slowly and aimlessly until a crossroads appeared ahead. For a moment, he hesitated.

If he went to the right, the road would wrap round and lead him home again. To the left would take him farther down the length of the island in the direction of the beach he had glimpsed from the boat.

The walk that had begun with no greater purpose than to give himself some breathing time suddenly acquired a more concrete goal. He turned left.

The sand was moist, the air brisk. He thrust his hands into his pockets and continued on down the path toward the beach.

Beyond the narrow rim of moonlit sand, the water glowed darkly. He stared out at it, thinking how absurdly peaceful it looked when it was anything but. The sea teemed with life and was roiled by energies humans could barely glimpse.

He walked on, enjoying the solitude. His body was pleasantly tired but his mind remained almost unnaturally active. He thought of Nickie and felt again the now familiar pang of yearning.

Resolutely, he continued until he reached the end of the path and stepped out onto the beach. Here all was silent except for the rhythmic whoosh of the waves. The night was so clear and the moon so bright that he could see a considerable distance in all directions.

A shape glowed whitely among the trees near the edge of the path. He stopped, puzzled, and looked more closely. It was far too large to be a rock, yet it didn't look like a boat, either.

Slowly he approached until he could make out the distinct contours of a small truck, the kind commonly used for hauling construction material.

Puzzled, he stood for a time, trying to imagine why anyone would park a truck in such a place. It occurred to him that he might have accidentally stumbled upon lovers, but if he had, he was as unaware of them as they must be of him. As far as he could tell, he was completely alone on the beach.

Why, then, the truck? Why here and now? Why placed back among the trees almost as though to hide it?

Frowning, he turned and stared out over the water. At first, he thought his eyes were playing tricks. The lights he thought he saw hadn't been there a few moments before. But as they became more distinct, he realized that a boat was approaching.

Quickly, obeying instincts he didn't quite understand, he stepped behind a nearby tree. The boat continued in toward shore. Within minutes, he could see it clearly.

It was a good-size trawler, perhaps thirty feet in length, the pilot house rising high above the water. Its roof bristled with antennae and a half-sphere radar dish.

The trawler moved in as close as the depth would allow, then paused, the engines idling. Several people emerged on deck. Conor heard voices but he could not make out the words.

One of the men climbed down the metal ladder into the water. Clouds moved across the moon as he splashed toward the beach. He was there, walking up the sand in the direction of the truck, before the clouds cleared enough for Conor to make out his face.

Ed. The builder's features were unmistakable. He wore a Windbreaker and khaki pants, but was hatless. As he neared the truck, the boat moved back out to sea. The sound of its engine died away quickly.

The truck started up. It bumped onto the path and disappeared toward the main road.

Nickie was still asleep when Conor got back to the cottage. He stripped off his clothes and slipped in beside her. She made a small sound of protest when his cold feet touched hers, but settled down in his arms quickly enough.

He lay, holding her, staring up at the rough-hewn ceiling. Dawn was creeping over the horizon before he slept again.

Chapter 13

Wearing one of Conor's shirts and nothing else, Nickie padded down to the kitchen. It was early morning. The air was crisp, tinged with the promise of autumn. She shivered slightly as she turned up the thermostat a notch.

She was mildly embarrassed not to have any memory of getting to bed. Obviously Conor had carried her up to the loft after their impassioned lovemaking. A faint flush stained her cheeks at the memory of that.

She shook her head in astonishment at her own unbridled behavior. All those years of containing her emotions within the pages of her books must have paid off in unexpected ways. She had virtually exploded.

In consideration of which, the least she could do was bring the poor man a recuperative cup of coffee.

She brewed a pot, then filled two mugs and carried them up the stairs. But when she got to the top, Conor was still so deeply asleep that she couldn't bring herself to disturb him. Instead, she tiptoed away.

Ten minutes later, having reclaimed her clothes and having determined that Conor was not stirring, she decided to leave. There were things she needed to do and, besides, a little time to herself felt more necessary than ever.

Quickly she penned a note to let him know where she had gone. As she let herself out the door, her gaze fell on the rug. She frowned slightly. Damp footprints stood out against the lighter color of the wool.

There was one set only and they appeared to be Conor's. It was a small matter, but she couldn't quite figure out how they had remained from the previous day.

By the time she reached Gull's Rest, Nickie had forgotten all about the footprints. She had other matters to occupy her, beginning with the news that she'd received a call from New York.

"Gentleman, it was," Donna informed her. She drew out the word as though it was a rarely deserved title. "Said he was terribly sorry to trouble me but if he could hear from you as quickly as possible, he'd be very grateful."

She looked at Nickie meaningfully. "He sounded so nice. You don't get that much these days. People are always in such a hurry. It's refreshing to speak with someone who's mannerly."

Nickie sighed. Without having to be told, she knew who Donna's phone friend had to be.

"I'll call him back," she promised, if only to get Donna to stop.

"He said quickly."

"Got it."

Donna stared at her. Nickie stared back. Finally, Donna made an exasperated sound and turned on her heel. But she had a parting shot. "Seems to me you'd be smart to hold on to a man like that 'stead of running after something you can't ever have." The kitchen door swung shut behind her before Nickie could muster a reply.

The guest phone was in a small alcove under the stairwell. Her hand shook slightly as she punched in numbers. As it began to ring, she took a deep breath and pushed the hurt as far down as she could. The odds were Donna was right, but she absolutely wasn't going to think about that now.

Moments later, Edward Harper was on the line. She could picture him sitting in his corner office, feet up on his desk, shirtsleeves rolled up. He was a handsome man in his forties, always elegant even when he cultivated a certain sincere dishevelment.

Edward had a black belt in karate, an M.B.A. from the Harvard Business School, a gold-plated reputation for publishing bestsellers and a lover named Dave. He was Nickie's editor and friend. She didn't like to let him down.

"All right," she said after they'd talked for a few minutes. "I suppose I could come down."

"Could? Darling, how many spots do you think there are on network morning TV? You've got a book popping next month, in case you've forgotten."

She hadn't, nor could she disagree with him about the importance of publicity. She just wished the opportunity had come at a better time.

"I know, I know. It's just that..."

"This is a rough time for you, I realize that." His sympathy was genuine; he'd lost a parent of his own the year before. "But maybe the best thing is to just get back in the saddle. Are you writing?"

"Not exactly." She was living instead, but this didn't seem the moment to say so.

"Then this will help you keep your hand in, at least on the business side. Besides, I thought you liked the Big Apple."

She did, at least in small doses, but not just now when everything was so tentative, so burgeoning with possibilities.

"I suppose..."

Edward was silent for a moment. Quietly he asked, "Is something wrong up there?"

"What makes you think that?"

"You don't sound like yourself."

Her laugh was shaky. "Who do I sound like?"

"I don't know— Look, seriously, if you need a shoulder—"

"I appreciate that, but maybe you're right. I just need to sort out a few things here. Will it be okay if I get there tomorrow?"

"That's cutting it a little close, but never mind. Just come as soon as you can."

They talked a little longer before Nickie hung up. She sat for a while staring into space, before leaving the alcove. Donna was nowhere in sight, for which she was grateful.

Her anxiety level was suddenly way up, out of keeping with the circumstances. The trip to New York didn't account for it. Halfway into a pair of clean slacks, she caught herself thinking about Conor. The thought of being parted from him even temporarily hurt terribly. What would it be like to say goodbye for good?

Pain stabbed through her. Leaving her face bare and her hair in a loose ponytail, she finished dressing and went back downstairs. Leaving the house, she walked briskly down the street. The Ellie Roberts Real Estate Agency was less than a block from the Gull's Rest, on the second floor of a weathered, blue-shingled building.

Nickie climbed the stairs to the door and knocked. Ellie herself answered. She was a small, trim woman with iron-gray hair, bright blue eyes, and a friendly but no-nonsense manner. Seeing Nickie, she didn't look surprised.

"Come on in," she said. "I just made some coffee. Want a cup?"

Nickie allowed as to how that would be welcome. They sat on the couch in front of the windows within sight of the water. Ellie smiled. "I thought you might stop by."

"I wasn't sure about it myself. Part of me just wants to put this off."

The older woman nodded. "That's understandable, but sometimes it's best to just get things finished with."

"How's the market?" Nickie asked with a wan smile. She didn't really care. Money wasn't the object. Closing the door on the past was.

"Not as good as a few years back, but better than it's been recently."

"Then I suppose I might as well go ahead."

They went over the details and Ellie got out a sales agreement. She would list the cottage at a price guaranteed to get attention. While she couldn't promise anything, she was confident it would go fairly quickly.

The formalities concluded, she refilled their coffee cups and regarded Nickie for a moment. Hesitantly she said, "I understand you live in Connecticut."

"That's right."

"Ever think of settling down here?"

Only constantly of late, but she wasn't about to tell Ellie that. Instead she tried hard to look surprised. "Why do you ask?"

"Just a stray thought. There's a fantastic piece of property on the market right now, priced very reasonably. The problem is finding a buyer."

Nickie's stomach turned over. She had a sinking feeling which piece of property Ellie was talking about. "Oh, where's that?"

"The old McDonnell place. Remember it?"

"Vaguely." Exactly, down to the last shuttered window.

"It's a knockout. Big but absolutely gorgeous."

That pretty much described its owner, too, but now probably wasn't the time to be thinking about that.

"Have you had any offers?"

"Several. The problem is Conor doesn't want to sell to a developer." Ellie sighed. "Of course, he'll probably have to in the end. You've met Ed Mulloney?"

"I ran into him the other day." The look on Nickie's face must have said it all. Ellie laughed. "He's been very persistent but I don't know—"

"Something wrong?"

"I really shouldn't be telling you this."

"My lips are sealed."

"There have been rumors that Ed's a little overextended."

"A little?"

Again, the older woman hesitated. Nickie could see her weighing the alternatives. On the one hand, she was trying to interest Nickie in the property. On the other, she was naturally reluctant to say anything that might come back to haunt her.

"He made a very good offer. Almost too good."

"And Conor turned it down?"

"Flat. Not that Ed seems discouraged. He appears to think he'll win out eventually."

"Then he's got financing from somewhere."

"I suppose," Ellie agreed.

The two women looked at each other. Nickie wasn't about to express an interest in Conor's house. That would be madness. But she was interested to know that Ellie thought it necessary to try to scare up another buyer.

The real-estate agent had been around a long time. If she thought there was something fishy about Ed Mulloney's financial situation, the odds were that she just might be right.

All of which was food for thought but didn't do much about the absence of breakfast. Nickie bit back a sigh. She was becoming such a physical creature, ruled by her appetites.

At home in Connecticut, she could live for a week on crackers and cheese gobbled in between writing bouts. But here she seemed to need something more substantial.

With so much on her mind, she didn't feel up to Norm's. Fortunately, there was an alternative.

Chapter 14

The grocery store had changed little from the way Nickie remembered it. A long, narrow space was filled to overflowing with rickety shelves. Open cartons were stacked on the floor, making passage between them almost impossible.

A plump, red-haired woman with a harassed expression was behind the counter. She was taking an order over the phone, jotting it down on the back of a brown paper bag. The fingers that held the stub of a pencil were yellowed from nicotine, the nails cracked.

"All right, I've got it. Yeah, I'll take care of it right away. Joey'll bring it over in about an hour."

She hung up with a sigh and glanced at Nickie. "That Georgina, she means well but sometimes she can be a real—" She broke off as she realized abruptly who she was speaking to.

"Why Nickie…Nickie Chandler. It is you, isn't it?"

Nickie allowed as to how it was.

Mabel Walters—of Walters Grocery & Tackle—looked at her narrowly. She had known Nickie's mother well, the two having been occasional drinking companions. Nickie supposed that Mabel was as close to a friend as Patty had possessed.

"You sure don't look much like your mom," Mabel said. She made it sound like Nickie's fault.

"I must take after my dad."

Mabel snorted. "Him? You should hope you don't. Going off and leaving her the way he did."

"He died," Nickie said.

"Same difference. Folks say you've done pretty well for yourself."

"Could be. How is Georgina these days?"

Mabel shrugged. "Same as always. Still expects everybody to jump when she says boo."

"She must be pretty old now," Nickie said, thinking of the woman who had taught her through most of elementary school. Georgina Samuels—strictly Miss Samuels to the cowed children who sat in her class—hadn't been any spring chicken back then. She had to be past eighty now.

"Too tough to die," Mabel said. She reached under the counter and pulled out a pack of cigarettes. With a grimace, she snapped the filter off one, stuck it in her mouth, and lit up.

"Can't abide these things," she said through the smoke. "My boy, Joey, keeps buying 'em. Says they're better for me." She tossed the discarded filter into the garbage. "Kids."

On impulse, Nickie said, "If Georgina wants her groceries now, I'll take them over."

Mabel looked at her narrowly. "Why'd you want to go and do that?"

Nickie smiled. She leaned a little closer to the counter as though about to impart a great secret. "To be nice."

Mabel chuckled. "Honey, you sure must have changed. Way I remember, you were a pretty tough cookie."

"Maybe I had to be."

Mabel took another drag on the cigarette and let it out slowly. She eyed Nickie through the smoke. "Yeah, maybe you did. Okay, tell you what, here's the list. You want to take care of it, be my guest."

Georgina Samuels still lived in the same small salt-box-style cottage just off the beach road. Carrying her groceries, Nickie made her way up the flagstone path.

The cottage was old and weathered but looked cheerful nonetheless. Late season mums bloomed in the window boxes and a friendly curl of smoke rose from the chimney.

The door was opened almost as soon as Nickie knocked. Georgina looked up at her with a delighted smile. "I thought that was you, child. Come in. I'm so pleased you've dropped by."

Nickie stepped inside, inhaling as she did the familiar fragrance of wood smoke, lemon oil and drying herbs. Georgina's house had always smelled of it. The same threadbare Oriental rugs lay over the softly gleaming plank floor. The same portrait of Georgina's sea captain grandfather held pride of place over the mantel.

Nothing at all seemed to have changed. Even Georgina herself was virtually the same. A little more stooped, perhaps, her hair a little whiter. But otherwise the same strong-willed, stout-hearted woman she had always been.

"What's that you've got?" she asked as she noticed the bag. "Now don't tell me Mabel Walters got you to deliver them?"

"I offered to do it," Nickie assured her. "I was planning to stop by, anyway. This just gave me a good excuse."

"Not that you'd ever need one," Georgina said as she took the bag and headed briskly down the hall that led to the kitchen. "Come along and I'll put on the tea. I just baked a nice lemon cake I'll bet you'll like."

Georgina had been baking the same lemon cake for at least the last twenty years. Nickie wasn't absolutely sure that it wasn't exactly the same cake since it had the consistency of a doorstop. Nobody had ever had the nerve to tell Georgina that she was a lousy cook.

"Thanks," Nickie murmured as Georgina set a generous slice in front of her. Maybe if she dipped it in the tea—

"You know, dear," Georgina said as she took the chair across from her, "I've followed your career with the greatest interest. Haven't missed a single one of your books."

Nickie stopped in mid-sip. She felt a flush creeping over her cheeks. "You haven't?"

Georgina grinned. "Every one. And you know something?" She leaned forward a little, her smile becoming confidential. "There's nothing new under the sun."

Nickie coughed and put her cup down hurriedly. After a moment, she laughed.

So much for preconceptions. Georgina Samuels, maiden schoolteacher and terror of the elementary school set, must have had a secret life somewhere along the line. She had also apparently enjoyed it.

"I'm glad to hear that," Nickie said. "Especially since you're the one who encouraged me to write." Softly she added, "The only one."

"I always knew you had it in you. It was obvious from the start." Georgina's eyes softened. "I'm not sure why, but sometimes the most creative people seem to be those who have gone through hard times growing up."

"You were also the first person who told me I could go to college," Nickie said. She laughed again. "At the time, I thought you were crazy."

"I don't blame you. But all that hard work certainly paid off."

"I had some luck, too."

"Maybe, but what you've got, you earned." Quietly, Georgina said, "I'm sorry about your mother."

"So am I."

That said, they moved on. Georgina filled her in on the latest news—the addition over at the school, the fancy computers they'd brought in, the handsome gym instructor who had the girls lined up to play field hockey, and so on. It was all good-natured and innocent.

Little by little, Nickie felt herself relaxing. Until, without warning, Georgina said, "Speaking of which, is it true what they're saying around town, that you and Conor have gotten back together?"

Nickie grimaced. She'd forgotten how impossible it was to have any privacy on an island this small.

"You know we'd all just love that," Georgina went on. At Nickie's surprised look, she went on, "Oh, yes, we would. There are plenty of people around here who thought the two of you were meant for each other."

Nickie doubted that strongly, but she didn't want to be rude. "I didn't realize anyone had given it that much thought."

"Dear, when you're basically cut off from the rest of the world for a good part of the year, people are bound to take a big interest in each other. I know some of us can seem no better than we have to be, but we're only human. Nobody's all good or all bad. It'd be awfully boring if we were."

"I suppose," Nickie said softly. She had to admit that Georgina had a point. What hurt she'd felt from gossip in the past had been very small compared to what had come directly from her sorrow at home.

While it was true people hadn't seemed to know what to do about Patty, some had reached out to her daughter. She'd been offered as many jobs as she wanted and when time came for her to leave, there'd been no lack of references for college and scholarships.

The encounter with Mabel Walters had reminded her of everything she hadn't liked about the island— the gossip, the lack of privacy, the constant, unrelenting assessing of other people's thoughts and behavior.

But, paradoxically, she was also reminded of all the good things that went hand-in-hand with that. Such as the genuine caring and concern, the willingness to help out a neighbor and even a stranger, the simple interest in other people that was the strongest badge of humanity.

"I guess this is a pretty good place," she said.

"I've never found a better one. But don't kid yourself, there's snakes in the grass here same as everywhere else."

Nickie's eyes met the old teacher's. There was something in the way Georgina said that—

"I suppose you know more about people around here than just about everyone else. You taught almost all of us over the years."

"That's the advantage of getting old," Georgina agreed. "You reach a point where nobody can put anything over on you."

"Has somebody been trying to do that?"

Georgina frowned. Weighing her words with care, she said, "Not me, personally. I'm small potatoes, after all. But I'm also part of this community and I can't say I like some of the things that are happening."

"Like what?"

"Like the overdevelopment. I agree with Conor on that. He was one of my best students, by the way. Same as you."

Conor had been two years ahead of Nickie in school. They'd never actually shared a class, but she'd been acutely aware of him all the same.

"What else don't you like?" she asked, if only to change the subject.

"I'm not sure," the older woman said softly. "There's just a feeling lately, something being out of whack. Know what I mean?"

"Maybe. Sometimes you can be used to a certain pattern and when it changes even a little, it kind of jumps out at you."

Georgina nodded thoughtfully. "That's just what I'm talking about. Now for instance, it used to be that the only time I had any sort of traffic going by my place late at night was during the summer when those damn fool tourists run all over creation. But just last night one of those little trucks went by real late. Whoever was in it sure was in a hurry to get home."

"It's quiet where I live in Connecticut, too," Nickie said. So quiet that she didn't disregard Georgina's interest.

The older woman nodded. "It was getting on for 3:00 a.m. I tend to sleep awfully lightly right about then. Goes with getting old. Funniest thing, too. I could have sworn when I looked out a while later, somebody was walking by. Now who'd be out for a stroll then?"

"I can't imagine." But in fact she could. There was a stray memory of icy cold feet against her own and those damp footprints on the rug.

Georgina looked at her narrowly. "Think hard, dear. I'm sure it'll come to you."

Nickie sighed. She felt as though she was in over her head and sinking fast. "He's a grown man," she said quietly. "He can take care of himself."

Georgina made a derisive sound and refilled their teacups. "He's a stubborn one, I'll give you that. But then he's had to be. Pretty much everybody he's cared about has let him down at one time or another."

Nickie's stomach clenched. She pushed her cup away and stared at Georgina. "It's hard to start trusting again when you've gotten used to getting along without it."

Georgina shrugged. She took a piece of the lemon cake and dipped it in her tea. "Good cake if you soften it up first. Try to bite it right off and you'll lose a tooth."

"You used to be more direct than that," Nickie said. But after a moment, she pulled her cup back and a moment after that she dunked the cake in.

Georgina was right, it wasn't bad if you went at it the right way. In fact, she might even get to like it after a while.

The problem was, would she get the chance?

Chapter 15

The Clamshell Café was, as usual, almost empty when Conor arrived. He glanced around, nodded at Norm, and strolled over to join the man already seated at the counter.

"How are you doing, Ed?" he asked quietly.

The developer glanced up. He looked startled and bleary-eyed, as though he'd had a rough night. "What? Oh, it's you. Just what I needed." He looked away, staring into his tomato juice, then suddenly turned back. "Come to your senses yet?"

"Afraid not." Norm ambled over, looking at both men cautiously. "Just coffee, please," Conor said.

Norm set a cup in front of him. Conor took a sip, waiting. It didn't take long. Ed was in a belligerent mood, itching for a fight.

"I gotta hand it to you," he said, "you're thick as they come. Nobody's ever gonna make you a better offer."

"Probably not," Conor agreed.

"I mean it. If you think holding out is gonna get me to up the ante, you're wrong."

"I don't think that."

"I don't get it," Ed said, shaking his head. "Your old man going down the tubes the way he did, you gotta be dead broke. If I was you, I'd sure as hell take the money and run."

"Maybe you would, but then I think the two of us see money differently."

"What's that supposed to mean?"

"You think it can buy anything and I know for a fact that it can't."

"Bull," Ed said. "I sweated blood for every dime I ever earned and lemme tell you something, I appreciate every single one of them. All that crap about money being the root of all evil was dreamed up by people like you to keep people like us from getting our fair share."

He took another swallow of his drink and grimaced. "Hey, Norm, dress this up for me."

Norm obliged but stingily. The vodka bottle barely made contact with the glass.

Ed laughed again. "Norm thinks I drink too much. Everybody's got an opinion, 'specially in this damned place." He sighed deeply. "You can't win in my business. If you don't build, nobody's got any work. But if you do build, everybody hates you for getting rich for bulldozing their favorite tree or some other crap."

He stared narrowly at Conor. "So what're you doing here anyway? How come you aren't out saving some friggin' whale?"

"I'm not actually in the whale end of the business. Water's more my speciality."

Ed sneered. "Maybe I ought to hire you next time I need a few wells dug. How strong's your back?"

"Strong enough, but it may take more than that. It's getting tough to dig wells around here. The water table's dropping."

"Baloney. All we need are a couple of good rainy seasons and we'll be fine."

Conor shrugged. "If you say so but weren't the wells a problem on that last condo development you did? The one down by the shore? I thought you really got held up on that."

Ed frowned, but he didn't deny it.

"Must have cost you a bundle."

"Damn straight it did."

"Couldn't have been easy to get money after that, 'specially with the banks tightening up the way they have. But you managed, didn't you? I hear you're building out on the Cape now, while you wait for something to open up here."

Ed put his glass down so that some of the liquid in it splashed onto the counter. He rounded on Conor. "How in hell do you know that?"

"Is there any reason I shouldn't?"

They stared at each other. Ed's face was flushed. His hand, as he reached for his drink again, was unsteady. "What the hell. It's no secret. A builder builds."

"And when he runs into trouble, when his credit line gets stretched too thin, he still finds a way to keep going."

It took Ed a minute to register that. When he did, his eyes glittered. "You accusing me of something?"

"Not yet."

The words hung between them. Ed took a long drink, emptying the glass. As he put it back down, he said, "You're nuts."

"Not usually. It's called illegal dumping, long-term pollutants with a high mortality factor for sea life. This is heavy-duty stuff. It tends to be used in processing building materials."

"So what? I don't even have a project going here right now. Thanks to you."

"No, but you've got the one on the Cape. What I'm wondering is if maybe I'm supposed to think that's where this stuff is coming from."

Ed muttered an expletive. "Like I said, you're nuts. First off, why should I even believe that this is actually happening? But if it is, who would be stupid enough to haul stuff all the way from the Cape down here? You got any idea what that would cost?"

"Illegal dumping's a big business. People pay plenty to get rid of stuff with no questions asked."

"Really? Gee, I didn't know that. Maybe I'm in the wrong line of work."

"Only if you don't mind looking at ten to fifteen in a federal pen."

"I'm not looking at anything, buddy, except a goddamn rich kid who can't get used to the fact that his family's not in charge around here anymore." He got off the stool, fished some money from his pocket and slammed it down on the counter.

Glaring, he said, "Stay out of my face, McDonnell. You go around making trouble for me and you'll find out what trouble really is."

The café door banged shut behind him.

Norm waited a moment before working his way down to the counter. Without being asked, he refilled Conor's coffee cup. "I don't know about that," he said.

"About what?"

"Been a long time since I went hunting, but when I did, I didn't exactly go out of my way to let the quarry know I was coming."

Conor smiled, but his eyes were cold. "How about when you go fishing, Norm. You take any bait with you?"

The older man looked at him for several moments. Softly he said, "Some great job you've got. I sure wouldn't want it."

"It's usually better than this," Conor said, but his voice lacked conviction. It was the now that mattered. He'd just opened the proverbial can of worms without being sure what was going to crawl out. Baiting Ed the way he'd done was a risk, but one he'd felt he had to take.

The thing was, he really didn't want anybody else getting involved. Anybody at all.

Especially not Nickie.

It bothered him that she hadn't been there when he woke up that morning. Her note had helped, but it didn't stop him from realizing how easily she'd slipped back into his life.

Too damn easily. He was a fool to let this happen. They'd only been apart a few hours and already he was looking forward to seeing her again so much that it almost hurt.

That wasn't good. He had a tough, dirty job ahead of him. He couldn't afford any distractions. And he sure as hell wasn't in the market for a major league weakness, a chink in the armor he'd built so carefully over the years and which he relied on more than he liked to admit.

He was still thinking about that when he left the café and headed back to the cabin. With Nickie so much on his mind, he was still surprised to find her waiting for him.

She was sitting in her car, but she got out as soon as she saw him. The no-nonsense swing of her hips as she walked toward him should have alerted him that something was wrong. But he was too busy thinking how good she looked to see what was coming.

"You," she said succinctly, "are crazy. You ought to be put some place where you can't hurt yourself."

"Hi, Nickie," he said, aware that he was smiling at her foolishly but not able to do much about it. It was just so good to look at her.

"Crazy," she repeated, exasperated.

He sighed and got out from behind the wheel. Gently, his long fingers touched her arm. "Let's talk about it inside."

"First," Nickie said when they had stepped into the cabin, "why didn't you tell me that Ed Mulloney was behind the dumping?"

Conor's eyebrows shot up. "Where on earth did you get that idea?"

"I called a friend of mine." The friend was the New York City Public Library, but she wasn't about to tell him that. It didn't seem an opportune moment to admit that some of her closest working relationships were with a bunch of research librarians she'd never actually met in the flesh.

"Just what did this friend tell you?" Conor demanded.

"That acetone is in paint thinners and varnish, so is ethanol, and formaldehyde is used as a wood preservative. All of which points in one direction—a construction project. And that means Ed Mulloney."

She took a breath and stared at him hard. This next part was shaky, but she was willing to give it a try. "The same Ed Mulloney you followed last night."

Conor paled. He looked flat-out spooked, which provided her with some satisfaction but not all that much. Thickly, he asked, "Just what makes you think that?"

"The footprints I saw on the rug this morning."

"No way. You couldn't possibly have put it together from something that slim."

"Oh, all right," Nickie admitted. "Georgina Samuels saw you."

Conor groaned. "Isn't there anything that goes on in this town without someone finding out about it?"

"No," Nickie said flatly. "Georgina's house is right on the road that goes to that little beach you were staring at so hard yesterday when we were out on the boat. She's at an age when she has trouble sleeping. Besides, it was the truck going by that got her attention. Ed's truck, right?"

"Maybe," Conor said, hedging.

"Which brings me to why I'm here."

His eyes crinkled. "You weren't just missing me?"

Horribly, but she wasn't going to be distracted. Not just yet. "If I was writing this in a book," she said, "Ed would be the villain. He doesn't care much about the environment and he probably could use the money. He's perfect."

"Hmm, maybe. Speaking of perfect—"

"Stop that," she murmured as his arms closed around her. He was so very warm and strong, so delightfully and excitingly familiar now and yet still so different from herself. Perfect—

"Don't," she said. It came out more as a plea than she'd intended.

Conor's searching mouth touched her throat. "It's been a long time since anybody worried about me. I kind of like it."

"Conor," Nickie gasped, making a halfhearted effort to pull away from him. The instant effect of his touch on all her senses was devastating. "Don't change the subject. I can help, I really can. If this is as bad as you think, you may not realize what you're up against."

Conor sighed. He raised his head and looked at her. Gently he said, "Sweetheart, there are half a dozen guys doing hard time in a federal prison in California who would find the idea that I need help real amusing. They might wish it was true, but they know better."

Nickie's eyes widened. "What are you talking about?"

"What being an environmentalist means these days. What did you think it was? All ivory tower fundraisers and talking to dolphins? I carry a U.S. Marshal's badge along with my Ph.D. and when I need to, I throw in a gun."

Her shock was unfeigned. She paled and a tremor ran through her. Who was this man she thought she knew? Not the golden prince of her youth, not the idealist she believed she'd rediscovered? A hard, tough man in a hard, tough world who wasn't afraid of danger and, indeed, seemed almost to court it.

Not someone she knew at all.

"I thought you were doing a coastal survey," she murmured.

"I was...I am. It's a good cover. In the years it's been ongoing, we've made some real progress identifying major pollution sites throughout this area and running down who's causing them. This is just one more."

Just one more. Another job, another challenge.

He held her a little away from him. Their eyes met. "It's my job, Nickie. It's what I do." A moment passed, another. He took a breath. His features were hard, his gaze shuttered. He seemed to have reached some decision in his own mind, one she'd been given no chance to help him make.

Quietly he said, "I work alone. You're not going to have any part in this. You can't. Understand?"

She did, too well. Last time, she'd been the one to say he couldn't have any part in what she needed to do.

There was a certain irony to the way things were turning out. She might even have been able to appreciate that if it hadn't hurt quite so much.

Chapter 16

"Kind of hot for this time of year, don't you think?" Edward drawled. They were seated in his office, he with his feet up on the desk, Nickie in the guest chair opposite him.

She'd been staring out the window for several minutes, lost in her own thoughts. Making polite conversation—which he ordinarily never did—was his way of reminding her that there was somebody else in the room.

"I'm sorry," she murmured. "What did you say?"

Edward swung his feet down and straightened in his chair. He looked at her bemusedly. "Kind of hot."

The city was enjoying a rare burst of Indian summer, one of nature's special graces that even concrete-and-steel dwellers had to sit up and notice.

But the beauty of the day, the harmony of life, the progress of the universe all flitted past Nickie unnoticed. Not even her successfully concluded appearance that morning on a network talk show had made much impact. She was strictly going through the motions and she knew it.

"Dear heart," Edward said more gently, "won't you tell me what the trouble is?"

"Trouble? What makes you think there's any trouble?"

"Only the fact that I have never seen you act this way. You are absolutely not yourself. What's the problem?"

"Nothing really. I guess I'm just feeling a little confused."

"About what?"

She hesitated. It wasn't in her nature to confide in other people, but Edward had always come through for her. He didn't deserve her sitting there like a bump on a log and not telling him why.

Slowly she said, "I'm not really sure what I'm doing here."

His eyebrows shot up. "You don't mean that literally, do you?"

Three years before, Nickie had happened to be in a room when a group of editors, forgetting her presence, had started talking about authors. The general thrust of the conversation was that people who spent a large part of their time in a world of their own making tended to be just a tiny bit eccentric. Or sometimes a big bit. It depended.

"Don't worry," she said, "it's not as bad as it sounds. It's just that I almost called you to tell you that I couldn't come."

"Heaven forfend. This was big deal publicity. What could possibly have kept you away?"

"The person I thought might want me to stay actually wanted me to leave. So it worked out fine anyway." She broke off, having said a great deal more than she'd intended.

Edward leaned back in his chair and studied her, not unkindly. At length, he sighed. "I want you to know that I would have put the money to good use."

"What money?"

"In the betting pool. But you see, I had it pegged for two years ago—spring of, to be exact—so I never even came close."

Nickie stared at him. She was very tired, not having slept at all the previous night, and all of a sudden nothing seemed to be making any sense.

"What betting pool?" she asked carefully.

"The one on when a certain person whom, I hasten to add, everyone here is very fond of, would find out that there was more to life than what goes on between the pages of a book."

Her eyes widened. He couldn't be serious. "You're not talking about me?"

He smiled. "I'm not?" Standing up, he reached for his jacket. "Come on."

"Where to?"

"Out and about. Sitting here in this stuffy office is making both our brains rot."

"It is stuffy, isn't it?" Nickie murmured as they waited for the elevator. She'd never really noticed it before but the air definitely smelled stale. "Don't they ever open a window around here?"

Edward shot her a chiding look. "How? Only way to do that is toss a chair through one."

Nickie shook her head in disgust. She'd never been bothered by the air before, not on all her trips to Edward's office. She'd never even noticed it. But now she seemed to notice everything. Every sense she possessed seemed acutely, inconveniently alive. She couldn't hide, no matter how hard she tried.

Stepping out on the sidewalk with Edward, she felt bombarded by the cacophony of noise. The pressing, churning mass of buildings and people all seemed to be shoving in against her. After the peace of the island, it was all but unbearable.

"Why the big sigh?" he asked.

Nickie hadn't realized she'd made a sound. She looked at him self-consciously. "I think I'm going through some kind of life crisis."

"You can't do that on an empty stomach. Let's get something to eat."

There was a rule in publishing—the size of the advance paid for a book had to exceed the price of the lunch at which it was discussed. Thankfully, Nickie had never had a problem with that, especially so, considering Edward's taste in cuisine.

They bought salt pretzels and root beer from a sidewalk vendor and consumed them while walking north toward Central Park. Fine food always inspired Edward. He began to wax philosophical.

"First off," he said, "you have to understand something about relationships. They roll along at their own pace, in their own direction. We're all just on for the ride."

"I think I just got detoured," Nickie murmured.

Edward shrugged the impressive shoulders that had helped carry his high school football team to a state championship. "Maybe, maybe not. The point is, you can't fight fate so why try?"

"That's your advice? I should just sit back and let whatever happens happen?"

"Of course not. You've got a brain, don't you? A good one. You also happen to have more gumption than most people I know. So use them. Follow your instincts, your heart, whatever you want to call it. Just don't sit around feeling sorry for yourself."

"That's not what I'm doing."

Edward ignored her and went on. "Most importantly, remember, you're not calling the shots this time around, at least not all of them. This one's for real, which means there's an honest-to-goodness other person involved, not some figment of your imagination. You've got to think of him."

"I am. I left, exactly as he wanted."

"Why do I have the feeling there's more to it than that?"

"Because you're an unusually perceptive man and a good friend?" Nickie asked softly.

Edward sighed. "Dear heart, I'm just a hard-bitten old editor who wants another book out of you. I've got a dreadful feeling I'm not going to get it until you solve this little problem. So how about it? Do it for me?"

"No," Nickie said with a smile.

"Right answer. Do it for you?"

"Possibly. I'm not sure."

"That's a beginning," Edward said. He took her arm and hooked it through his. Together, they proceeded on up the avenue.

Chapter 17

Conor grimaced as he rubbed the back of his neck. He had been crouched in the same position for so long that it was probably pointless to even try to get the kinks out of his body. So far the surveillance of Mulloney Development was going by the book which was to say it was tedious, uncomfortable and uneventful.

He was playing it absolutely straight. No heroics, which weren't in his line anyway. He'd put in a call to the head office, telling them what he suspected and alerting them to the possible need for backup. Now all he had to do was wait.

And wait.

The night had turned cooler. He pulled his Windbreaker more closely around him and tried hard not to think about what he might be doing instead. Nickie featured prominently in those thoughts, but then, she was always there, hovering in the back of his mind.

He frowned. His last sight of her, as she'd walked out of the cabin, was hard to take. He'd done what was right, but he had to keep reminding himself of that. She couldn't get involved in what he was doing. It was simply too dangerous for them both. He had to keep his mind clear and she . . .

She had to be kept safe.

The door of the headquarters office opened. Conor stiffened. Ed was coming down the stairs. His walk was unsteady. It looked as though he'd been drinking. Hard.

The Jeep was parked fifty feet away, back in the woods. By the time Conor reached it, Ed's Caddy was roaring out of sight. Conor kept to a safe distance as Ed turned in the direction of town.

Barely five minutes later, he pulled up in front of the island's package store, got out of the car and went in. He returned almost immediately, carrying a bag.

Conor watched as he got behind the wheel, unscrewed the top on a bottle and took a long swallow. There was a look of desperation on his face as he put the bag down on the seat next to him and switched on the ignition.

Conor muttered an expletive. He hesitated barely a split second before ramming his foot down on the accelerator.

When the Jeep suddenly swerved in front of him, Ed blinked in surprise. His normal reaction time wasn't bad but alcohol dulled his reflexes. He was still sitting there staring when Conor walked up to the door on the driver's side and opened it.

"Come on, Ed," he said quietly. "I'm giving you a lift."

"What in hell...?"

Before he could go any further, Conor said, "Look, this has got nothing to do with anything except the fact that you've got no business driving right now. Be smart. I'll drop you off wherever you want to go."

Even as he spoke, he was only too well aware that he was screwing up. He was a professional, Ed was the mark. This wasn't how it was supposed to be.

The problem was he just didn't seem to have any choice. In his current condition, Mulloney was a potentially lethal weapon. Conor couldn't just stand back and wait for him to go off.

"If thish is some kinda trick..." Ed began.

"It isn't," Conor said. "Come on."

"Wait..." Staring at him bleary-eyed, Ed said, "You sherious?"

Conor nodded. "Dead serious."

"That's funny," Ed said. He started to laugh as he fumbled for the armrest that separated the two front seats. "But let's take my car. I can't 'ford to be seen in that heap you drive. Gotta think of my reputation, you know."

He was still laughing as he slid across the seat to the passenger side, clutching the bag along with him.

Not sure who he was more disgusted with—himself or Ed, Conor got behind the wheel.

* * *

An hour later, Conor returned the Caddy to the parking lot next to the package store. Ed could pick it up there whenever he got around to it, which, by the look of things, wouldn't be real soon.

About to get into the Jeep, he hesitated. The idea of heading home alone didn't hold much appeal. He already knew he was going to have trouble sleeping.

There was a small newsstand just down the block. He could get a newspaper, maybe a couple of magazines, catch up with what was going on in the world. Think about something other than Nickie.

Except for the girl behind the counter, the newsstand was empty. She gave Conor a vague smile and went back to the book she was reading.

The book had a flowery sort of cover. There was a woman on it, and a man. They were embracing.

On impulse, he asked, "What kind of book is that?"

The girl glanced up, startled. She flushed slightly. "A romance."

Think about something other than Nickie. Fat chance.

"Do you have any books by Nickie Chandler?" Maybe she wouldn't. It was a stupid idea, anyway. Men didn't read those books and he certainly didn't want to. He couldn't figure out why he'd even asked.

"Oh, sure," the girl said brightly. "We've got all of them."

She bounced out from behind the counter, gave him a long look, and said, "Here, let me show you."

Chapter 18

His sculpted arms surrounded her with infinite tenderness. Gently but implacably, she was drawn into his embrace. Candlelight flickered over the burnished muscles of his bared chest. Beyond the castle walls, a north wind blew but Lady Chandra did not feel it. Nothing existed for her but the passion and power of her own lord's desire. Timidly, for she had never known a man in such a way, she reached a hand down to—

Holy cow. Sitting bolt upright in bed, the covers drawn over his own bare chest, Conor stared at the book in amazement. He'd had no idea.

All those years going into bookstores and other places where these things were sold—and come to think of it they seemed to be sold everywhere. All those years of vaguely knowing they existed, but never so much as glancing at one.

What was it Freud had asked—"what do women want?" He could have saved himself a whole lot of trouble by picking up a couple of romances.

He turned to the next page, saw that Lady Chandra and her lord were still hitting it off, and sighed again. To be fair, the book was well written. He had to give Nickie that.

It appeared to have interesting characters and an actual plot. But it also had a great deal of rather detailed . . . romance.

All right, sex.

"They're going at it like bunnies," he muttered, turning another page. Either Nickie had one hell of an imagination or she was a whole lot more experienced than he'd guessed.

That last possibility hurt enough to make him suck in his breath. He frowned and kept reading. Halfway through the chapter, the penny dropped.

The guy's name was Conor.

A slow smile spread across his face. He set the book aside and reached for another. No Conor here, but definitely a Donnell. As in McDonnell?

Or here, in yet another book, no Conor or Donnell, but a Padraic. Padraic was Conor's middle name.

Well, how about that?

Things were looking up. He was feeling better than he had since she'd left the cabin with that hurt look in her eyes.

Jeez, he could have handled that better. He liked to think of himself as kind of a sensitive guy but he'd sure made a hash of it where Nickie was concerned.

She was the sensitive one. Look at the books she wrote, all about true love and moonlight, idealism and happy endings. If she didn't believe at least some of that stuff, she couldn't be so convincing about it.

And he'd sent her packing—twice.

Nice going, Conor. Not the one in the book, who was doing fine for himself, but the one who had to live in the real world and at the moment wasn't enjoying it much.

It wouldn't hurt to tell her he'd just wanted to keep her safe.

He turned over and glanced at the clock beside the bed. It wasn't that late. Donna would get her back up if she had to answer the phone at such an hour, but he could get around that.

Quickly, he rose and dressed. The cabin was only a quick drive from the Gull's Rest. He parked half a block away and walked down the street.

When he'd driven Nickie back a few nights before, he'd watched to make sure she got in safely. He'd seen the lamp go on in her room and a moment later, watched as she pulled the curtains shut.

But now that room was dark. She must have turned in early. Still intent on avoiding Donna, he picked up a pebble and tossed it lightly at the window. It clinked against the glass without damage and fell back to earth.

Nothing. He tried again.

Again nothing.

Either Nickie was deeply asleep or she wasn't there.

Then where was she? The island's night spots didn't stay open once the summer season was over. The big old Victorian hotel near the dock was still operating and it had a bar, but he had a hard time picturing her there.

Could she be at the Clamshell? The café was usually closed at this hour, but you could never tell with Norm. Sometimes he just decided to stay open.

Conor was thinking about going over there when he decided to try once more. This time he used a slightly larger pebble and loped it just a bit more firmly.

Just enough to break the glass.

A light flashed on above the porch. Donna yanked the door open. *"What's going on out there?"*

Conor sighed. If he'd been eleven years old, he might have thought about skedaddling. But he wasn't and he didn't—at least not much.

"Mrs. Woodward," he said as he stepped out of the shadows, "I've broken one of your windows. I'm sorry and I'll be glad to replace it."

Donna pulled her pink chintz bathrobe more snugly closed across her bosom and glared at him. "Conor? Conor McDonnell?"

"Yes, ma'am. As I said, I'm sorry about the window. I'll—"

"Just what do you think you're doing?"

"I didn't want to disturb you and I didn't realize Miss Chandler was asleep." It sounded as dumb as it felt.

"You were trying to get Nickie Chandler's attention?" Donna seemed delighted by the notion and why shouldn't she? It was a great piece of gossip. Conor McDonnell acting like a lovesick boy throwing pebbles at Nickie Chandler's window. Dumber than dumb.

"Something like that. About the broken pane—"

"Send Dan over from the gas station tomorrow. He takes care of things like that for me."

She was letting him off easy. He had to wonder—why?

"By the way," Donna said, "Nickie isn't here. She left yesterday."

As body blows went, it wasn't the worst he'd ever taken. But it was close.

Only one thing kept him on his feet—the cold, hard knowledge that it was no more or less than what he'd secretly expected.

She'd walked out on him once before with a whole lot less encouragement than he'd given her this time around.

And she wasn't alone. His mother had walked out on his father. Nor had it stopped there. His father had escaped into death rather than admit to his son how he had betrayed him.

With all that experience behind him, Conor shouldn't have any trouble dealing with this. No trouble at all.

Only the pain exploding inside him said otherwise.
That and the icy rage that gnawed at the edges of his
soul and grew with each passing thought of the woman
who had left him so nakedly alone.

Chapter 19

His noble features were taut with arrogance as the Duke eyed his fractious wife. He strode across the drawing room and seized her by the shoulders, crushing her in his embrace. . . .

That was terrible. The duke was coming across as insensitive, brutish and not too bright. In short, not remotely suitable for the lead role in a romance.

Nickie sighed and pressed the delete button. Her entire morning's work was wasted and with it her attempt to get started on a new book.

All of which just went to show what happened when she tried to work with a hero named Desmond.

Or when she tried to work at all. She'd had trouble writing down a list of errands she needed to run.

Clearly, a big chunk of her brain was simply refusing to cooperate.

Perhaps she should have stayed in New York. In the anonymity of a hotel room, she might have been able to think better. But she'd craved the safe familiarity of her own home, thinking she would find solace there.

It wasn't working out that way.

For the second night in a row, she had slept poorly. Her eyes burned, she couldn't get herself to eat anything and she felt a distressing tendency to burst into tears without warning.

If she had been one of her own heroines, she'd have thought she was pining.

But she wasn't one of those nice, innocent—although strong-willed—young women she wrote about. She was completely different.

Wasn't she?

Well, no, it seemed she wasn't. Try though she did, she couldn't seem to think of anything other than Conor and the way they had parted.

He'd said that she couldn't have any part in what he had to do. She'd claimed to understand, but in fact she'd been truly hurt. Enough to go off to New York without telling him.

She regretted that now. It had been childish. But the truth was, she'd been afraid that if she did tell him where she was going, he might not care.

He might even be relieved.

Sweet heaven, her self-confidence was about as low as she could ever remember it getting. And considering what she'd been through in her life, that was really saying something.

Was that what loving Conor did to her? Made her doubt everything she had accomplished and become? Made her success, her independence, the whole structure of her life seem somehow inconsequential?

If that was love, it could stay between the pages of her books where dealing with it was a whole lot safer.

Except it didn't seem inclined to remain caged there anymore. In fact, it seemed bent on running wild.

Heaven help her.

She pushed her chair away from her desk, giving up the pretext of working. From the window beyond where her computer was set up, she could see the garden. The leaves were ablaze with color. Squirrels darted about busily as small, tuft-headed birds flitted back and forth.

The house wasn't large but it was comfortable. Maybe too much so. She'd gotten in the habit of simply being there, following the same routine day in and day out, hardly venturing beyond the confines of the nearby town unless she absolutely had to.

Surely that wasn't a healthy way for a woman her age to be living. She should be more involved, have more friends, date, something.

Instead she had sought solitude and, to a large measure, she had found it. Such a reaction wasn't all that unusual for someone with her background, but now it no longer seemed to suit her.

She could call Conor.

The thought rose unbidden in her mind. There was a phone at the cabin, she'd seen it. Odds were the number was listed.

Call him and say what? That she'd had to go to New York for the TV appearance and was taking some time at home to start a new book? That when he'd wrapped up the dumping problem, he might think about coming down to Connecticut for a bit?

If he was in the mood, that was. Keep it casual, no pressure on either of them. Wasn't that how relationships were supposed to be these days?

She hated this. It was all so shallow and phony, people pretending that they didn't really care about much of anything because to admit otherwise might mean opening themselves up to hurt.

It was never like that in her books. There people took risks; they dared, they lived life to the fullest.

Not like her, safe in her little house, in her little world, behind all the nice, neat walls she'd made for herself.

On the other hand, she could call and apologize for leaving without telling him where she was going. What was the worst thing that could happen?

That he might not have realized she had left?

Before she could talk herself out of it, she picked up the phone.

"Sure thing," Dan said. "I'll stop by Donna's place this morning and take care of it."

Conor nodded. He ignored Dan's broad grin and gunned the Jeep. "Send me the bill."

"You bet," Dan said. He was trying real hard to look serious but he wasn't having much luck. The story about Conor McDonnell standing outside Nickie Chandler's window like some lovesick teenager had obviously already made the rounds. If the look on Dan's face was anything to go by, it wouldn't be forgotten any time soon.

Conor pulled back out onto the road and headed south. It was still early but the coffee would be poured at the Clamshell and the pancakes would be flipping. He was hungry, but not enough to put up with the good-natured scrutiny he'd undoubtedly get from the fishermen who gathered there before taking their boats out.

Besides, he had work to do.

On the way to it, he decided to drive by Ed's place, where he'd dropped the builder off the previous night. It was one of the cluster houses Ed had put up on a bluff overlooking the harbor. That development had been finished a scant six years before but already the space between the houses and the cliff's edge was a good dozen feet less than it had been.

Slowly but surely, the bluffs along that side of the island were eroding. The houses were well constructed, he'd give Ed that, but long before they reached the end of their normal life span the waves would take them.

He wondered if the people who had bought them yet realized that or if they were just reluctant to admit it even to themselves.

There was no sign of life in Ed's house. He was probably still sleeping it off. That suited Conor fine. He had no wish to keep baby-sitting the developer. Ed was nervous enough already. Sooner or later, he'd do something stupid and trip himself up.

Back at the cabin, Conor loaded his gear into the boat and set out. It was cold on the water. The wind whipped his hair and made his skin burn.

At the site where he'd taken the samples, he killed the engine. The boat began drifting. He got out the small, portable lab he'd brought along and began filling vials.

He worked for almost an hour, all the while doing his damnedest not to think of Nickie. But the image of how she had looked, all wind-blown and bright-cheeked, working alongside him, kept intruding.

His face was grim by the time he finished and turned the boat back toward shore. He was just tying up at the dock when the phone rang in the cabin.

The wind was blowing too hard for Conor to hear it.

Chapter 20

Nickie set the receiver down slowly but continued to stare at the phone. She didn't know whether to be disappointed or relieved that Conor wasn't answering. He was undoubtedly out working, doing exactly what he'd wanted to be free to do without interference. She should be glad.

Except that she wasn't. Even as she forced herself to walk away from the phone, go into the kitchen and make a cup of tea, she felt a rising tide of anxiety.

Where was he? What was he doing?

Was he in danger?

This was crazy. He was a grown man who had given her every reason to believe that he could more than take care of himself. He'd made it abundantly clear that he didn't want her getting in the way.

She sat at the kitchen table and sipped the tea without tasting it. Ed Mulloney was a fool. Conor would be more than a match for him. She'd wait and try calling him again. Maybe suggest that Connecticut trip. Nice and casual.

She got up, went over to the sink and dumped the tea out. In her office, she switched the computer off and put the answering machine on.

It was cold outside. She could feel the dampness even through the bulky sweater she was wearing. She got into her car and sat for a moment, her hands on the wheel.

She could drive to the store, pick up a few supplies, come home and light a fire. Maybe then she'd be in the mood to work.

She could go buy a needlework kit and actually do it.

She could clean the house... take a nap... watch a video... plan next year's garden.

Get a dog... a cat... a parakeet. All three.

She could play it safe.

Or she could follow her heart.

It was late afternoon when Nickie maneuvered her car onto the island ferry. Clouds scudded across the sky and the wind was picking up.

"Good thing you're going over today," the young woman who took her ticket said. "We might not be running tomorrow."

"Is the weather turning that bad?" Nickie asked. She remembered times when the island had been cut off for days.

The young woman shrugged. "Who knows? The forecasts only seem to be right half the time, if then. But it sure seems like it's getting set to do something."

She was right, Nickie realized as she left her car on the lower deck. There weren't many passengers but what few there were clustered in the enclosed area around the food counter. Most were holding steaming cups of coffee or hot chocolate.

She took a seat on one of the hard benches and looked out through the wide plate-glass windows at the water. It was the color of steel below white caps that appeared to grow higher as she watched.

The crossing was rougher than she'd expected. She'd never been subject to sea sickness but once or twice she'd come close. This time she thought she might again.

She breathed a sigh of relief when the island jetties finally came into sight through the gathering fog. Even so, waves were pounding against the breakwater and the wait to off-load her car seemed to drag on forever. As she drove onto the dock, she tried hard not to think of Conor and his snug cabin.

Donna opened the door in answer to her ring. She did a long, slow double-take and smiled.

"Well, well."

Nickie stepped inside. "I did mention I'd be returning."

"That's true, you did."

"Anything interesting happen while I was gone?" She really wasn't in the mood for polite chitchat, but it was better to let Donna get it out of her system.

"Nothing much. A little accident with a window. That's all."

Nickie frowned. Donna looked insufferably pleased with herself and she couldn't figure out why. But she was also absurdly disappointed that there was no mention of Conor. She couldn't flat out ask if he'd come by, but if he had, surely Donna would mention it.

No such luck.

"Getting windy out there," Nickie said as she moved toward the staircase.

"Might get some rain tonight."

Again, she thought of the cabin near the shore and felt a piercing sense of longing.

"I guess I'll go up."

"You do that," Donna said. Before Nickie had her foot on the first tread, the older woman disappeared through the door to the kitchen. A moment later, Nickie heard her pick up the phone.

In no hurry to hear whatever it was Donna might be saying, she went on up to her room. It was dark and felt chilled. She switched the lamps on and put a hand to the radiator. It was warm, there was definitely heat coming up.

Slowly she looked around. The room seemed unchanged from when she had left it except for—what was that? A dusting of white particles under the window caught her eye. She bent down and touched them. Her fingers came away slightly sticky.

Some sort of putty. She looked up. One of the windowpanes looked newer than the others. That must have been what Donna was talking about.

The small mystery solved—she presumed—she unpacked. The room had warmed up but she still felt chilled. What she needed was a nice, long hot shower and then to bed. Alone.

The shower creaked and complained, but eventually it did heat up. She stood under it, luxuriating as the tension of the long day eased from her. It didn't disappear entirely, but by the time she got out and wrapped herself in a towel, she was feeling much better.

Too much, in fact, to contemplate turning in.

A glance out the window showed that while the wind was still definitely blowing, it hadn't yet started to rain. Nor was it particularly cold.

She could go for a walk, work off some of the nervous energy that suddenly seemed to be flooding her, and then—at long last—get a good night's sleep.

Wrapped in a bulky Irish sweater, her hair quickly done up in a French braid, she slipped out of the inn. The wind caught her at once and blew her up the street, an encouraging but not unpleasant presence at her back.

At this hour only a few stragglers were still out and they seemed intent on getting home as quickly as possible. Vowing not to go far, Nickie continued on around the corner, past the small library and along the road that led past the post office toward the beach.

The night was exhilarating. She had forgotten how much she enjoyed nature in all its fine fettle glory. It had a way of blowing out the cobwebs and putting everything in proper perspective.

There was still no sign of rain and in the time she'd been out the wind hadn't increased. She'd probably be all right if she spent just a few minutes on the beach.

Even through her shoes, the sand was cold and wet. She stood, arms wrapped around herself, and watched the furious, foamy waves pound against the sand. The rhythmic pulse of the sea was far louder than usual. It roared in her ears, blocking out all thought, all doubt.

She kept going. It wasn't smart, she'd regret it the moment she had to turn around and head back, but the wild night released a desperate yearning in her. She had spent too much of her life trying to be safe. It was time to be free.

Which was all well and good but that didn't keep her from shivering as the damp night air crept inexorably beneath her sweater. She had to turn back. It was crazy to be out in this.

Yet the sheer power of the approaching storm entranced her. She felt taken out of herself, caught up in a primal force unlike any she had ever known except with—

Oh, no, she wasn't going to think of Conor. She had come out into the night and the storm to clear her mind of him. She wanted to sleep without dreams, to wake refreshed and better able to face whatever the day might bring.

This rite of walking along the beach pounded by waves and wind was a kind of exorcism. She would not give it up.

The lights of town faded behind her. Ahead, the beach curved away into darkness. Nickie hesitated. Already she had come much farther than she'd intended.

Even as she debated what to do, the wind increased. The first lashings of rain fell against her upturned face.

The decision made for her, she reversed her course and set out back the way she had come. But the wind suddenly seemed a wall. She bent slightly, hunching her shoulders, and pushed into it.

It gave, but only grudgingly and with great effort. Before she had gone more than a few yards, she was already feeling the strain. The wet, heavy sand tugged at her feet, the wind tore at her, slicing right through her sweater, and the rain was becoming heavier by the moment.

The lights of town, which a few minutes before had seemed not so very far away, suddenly seemed unreachable.

She would have to climb up the dunes to the road. It would be easier going there—not easy, but easier.

Except that when she tried to climb, the wind pushed her back, like hands tugging at her. She slipped once, then again. The second time, she rolled all the way to the base of the dune, coming up spitting sand and fighting for breath.

This was ridiculous. She was exhausted and hurting, and she had barely gone any distance at all. Worse yet, the storm was increasing.

Obviously coming out had been a terrible mistake. But realizing that did her no good at all. She simply had to get back.

Once more, she struggled up the dune and by dint of grabbing hold of the few scraggly bushes that grew along it, she managed to finally pull herself to the top. But by the time she got there, she was bruised and cut. Her hands were actually bleeding and somewhere along the way, she'd gotten whacked in the head hard enough to start a bruise forming on her brow.

Rain coursed down her face, mingling with the few tears of fright and frustration that would not be denied. She brushed them aside angrily and tried to straighten up.

It was better on the road, she'd been right about that. But it wasn't much better. Her footing was surer, but the wind still pounded her unmercifully and the rain was now falling so heavily that she could barely see in front of her.

Soaked to the skin, her hands stinging and her head throbbing, Nickie put one foot blindly in front of the other. She had no choice but to keep going. Already, the temperature was dropping. If she remained outside much longer, she would be in even more serious trouble.

Yet even as she told herself that she'd never do anything so foolish again in her life, her strength was going fast. The nights without sleep, the worry and confusion, were all taking their toll.

Grimly, she pushed on, but with each step, the cost grew. Her breathing became labored. Rain blurred her vision and all the while, the wind howled, mingling with the crash of the waves that in places were beginning to wash up onto the road.

No mere storm this, but a full-blown nor'easter that would cut across the island with a vengeance. And she was right out in the worst of it, alone and unprotected.

Chapter 21

Conor leaned forward, struggling to see through the rivulets of rain washing over the windshield. The storm was worsening far more quickly than he'd expected.

He'd finished work in the afternoon, then had decided, on the basis of the weather forecasts, to check on his family's house. After several hours of securing shutters across the windows and generally battening the place down, he'd realized that he needed to pick up a few supplies. He'd gotten to the grocery store just as Mabel was closing up but she'd let him in to grab what he needed.

Now, finally, he was on his way home. In the nick of time, it seemed. He'd been through a lot of storms on the island. This one didn't look to be anywhere near as bad as some. But neither was it anything to be out in.

So what the hell was that person right up ahead of him doing?

His headlights caught the shape of someone bent over, walking into the wind, just as he came around a curve in the road. Automatically, he swerved to give himself more room.

With the road already as wet as it was, he couldn't just hit the breaks. But he did slow to a stop a few dozen yards past and back up.

Rolling down the window, he peered into the storm-roiled darkness. *"Nickie?"*

It couldn't be. He was hallucinating out of some mixture of desire and anger. She couldn't possibly be here, walking alone, through the storm.

"Conor." The way she said his name, so filled with joy and relief yet also mingled apprehension, shattered any thought that she was an illusion. This was a flesh-and-blood woman, soaking wet, buffeted by the wind, yet still incandescently beautiful.

And infuriating.

Hardly aware of what he was doing, he got out of the Jeep and stalked toward her. His voice rose above the wind, hard and iron-edged. "What in hell are you doing here?"

Nickie took a quick step back. She wasn't afraid—precisely. Just cautious. The storm tore at him, but he seemed oblivious to it, standing there tall and indomitable, his chiselled features tautly drawn and his eyes alight with emotions she didn't care to recognize.

"Walking," she said.

He stared at her as though she had taken leave of her senses. "Walking? You came out in this to *walk?*"

She made a small, placating gesture. "I didn't realize it would get this bad so quickly."

Conor stared at her. He shook his head slowly. "You didn't realize— What kind of answer is that? You aren't even supposed to be here." He stepped back a pace, the better to see her. Remorselessly he said, "You left."

So much for the fear that he might not have noticed, she thought. He had and he was clearly none too pleased about it. Truth be told, he looked furious.

The storm that had begun to frighten her no longer seemed so bad. Maybe she'd be smart to prefer it to Conor in his present frame of mind.

"I'm heading back to town," she said, "and you're going in the opposite direction so I'll just be on my way—"

He made a sound deep in his throat that sounded uncannily like a growl. In the next instant, her feet went clean out from under her. Ignoring her protests, he lifted her easily into his arms and carried her toward the Jeep.

"This really isn't necessary," Nickie insisted even as she struggled to ignore the sudden rush of pleasure that went through her at his touch. "It's not that bad. I'm sure I can get back without—"

"Shut up," Conor said.

Her eyes widened. She couldn't remember him ever being rude before.

"What did you say?"

He tossed her into the passenger seat and was about to shut the door on her side. Instead, he paused for just a moment. His head lowered, dark against the storm-swept sky.

"I said, shut up." As though to enforce the command, he laid his mouth hard on hers. The kiss was over in an instant but the effect lingered. There had been no gentleness in his touch, only raw, male mastery.

Silently she touched her fingers to her lips. Given the circumstances—and the fact that he seemed to be holding on to his temper by a hair's breadth—it just might be smarter to do as he said. No word passed between them as Conor got in beside her, gunned the motor and headed back down the road.

Away from town.

"We're going the wrong way." The circumstances be damned, she wasn't about to let him run roughshod over her. Never mind that her heart was beating frantically and the hot thrumming of blood in her veins made it all but impossible to think. She still wasn't going to let this happen.

"No," Conor said without looking at her. "We're not."

"I checked back in at the Gull's Rest."

"That's nice."

"It's late and the storm will only get worse. I really think—"

Very quietly, Conor said, "Nobody with the sense of a gnat would have come out walking in this. That being the case, what you think doesn't carry a whole lot of weight."

His derision stung her. She stiffened. "Oh, I see. You've never done anything you regretted?"

Conor cast her a single, cutting look. "Don't get me started, lady. Just sit back and enjoy the ride. We'll be there in a couple of minutes."

She sat, but only because she had no choice. The Jeep pushed on through the night and the storm. The wind howled and the rain grew even heavier.

Nickie couldn't even see the turnoff that led to the cabin but Conor found it unerringly. He pulled up in front, away from any of the trees, and got out.

She went to do the same but before she could put a foot on the ground, he lifted her again and carried her up the path. She would have objected—really, she would—but her head was muffled against his broad shoulder and she couldn't see to get her bearings.

With one hand Conor unlocked the door and stepped inside. He kicked it shut behind him and carried Nickie into the main room.

Sturdy log walls blocked out the sound of the storm. In the relative silence, her ears rang. She had the sudden, dazed feeling of her life spinning out of control and had no idea what to do about it.

Conor set her down on the couch without a word and went over to light the fire. It had already been laid and caught instantly. The scent of wood smoke began drifting up the stone chimney.

Nickie shivered. For the first time, she let herself realize how thoroughly wet and uncomfortable she was. The storm had soaked her through. Her clothes clung to her and her hair was a sodden mass.

If she stayed where she was, she'd ruin the couch and the rug under it. Unsteadily, she rose. She had some idea about making her way to the bathroom and wringing herself out, but the cabin seemed vaguely out of balance and her legs were unaccountably weak. She swayed and had to catch hold of the couch to keep from falling.

Conor finished with the fire and turned. He glared at her. "Stay where you are."

She shook her head. It felt absurdly heavy. As though from a great distance, she heard her voice. "I'm all wet. I'll ruin—"

His hands were hard and demanding as they closed around her arms. In the darkness of the cabin, there seemed to be only the fire dancing high and the burning light in his eyes. She was drawn against him, the heat of his body warming her, chasing out fear, dissolving doubt.

She trembled, not knowing whether to laugh or cry. Her senses whirled. She had meant to go slow, to think twice, not to rush anything. But now it was all coming crashing down on her and she couldn't seem to do anything about it.

"Take off your clothes," Conor said, far away, down the deep tunnel her senses were slipping into. Making no sense. He couldn't mean—

"Not here." It was all she could get out, but it was enough. He said something harsh and angry, and took hold of her sweater.

She meant to stop him, but her strength failed and perhaps the will to do so hadn't been there to begin with. In an instant the sweater was stripped from her and tossed onto the floor. Her slacks followed quickly. He bent, removing her shoes and socks, then stood again, his body brushing the length of hers as he rose.

She stood, shivering in no more than the lacy scraps of her bra and panties. The cabin was suddenly freezing cold. Nickie trembled convulsively and raised her hands to cover herself.

"Go away," she said. The words rang between them, weighted by a world of desperation and doubt. He flinched but did not relent. His long fingers, callused at the tips, brushed the curve of her breasts as he reached for the front clasp of her bra.

"No." Angry now, and also afraid, she tried to slap his hands away. But he would have none of it.

His face grim, his eyes shuttered, he stripped the garment from her. A faint groan broke from him as he stood back for a moment, gazing at her.

Slowly she raised her head and met his gaze. The torment in his eyes shocked her. He looked like a man fighting for his life.

Forgetting her own distress, she reached out to him.

Chapter 22

At the first touch of her hands on his skin, Conor knew he was lost. Honesty forced him to admit that he had been from the moment he came upon her in the storm.

All the anger he'd felt when he'd learned she had left dissolved before the sheer, overriding force of his hunger for this woman. She was as necessary to him as life itself.

Slowly he cupped her face, his thumbs tracing the delicate bones beneath pale, damask smooth skin. Her eyes were wide and luminous, her lips slightly parted.

He thought of the way he had kissed her in the Jeep and winced. At the same moment, he saw the bruise on her forehead. His finger traced it lightly as he demanded, "What happened? How did you get this?"

She swallowed with some effort and murmured, "I don't know... wait, on the beach. I fell climbing the dunes... I think." Her voice trailed off. She sounded uncertain, confused, and utterly exhausted.

Pain filled him—and fear—at the thought of what she had gone through. For an instant he allowed himself to consider what else might have happened if he hadn't come along when he had. But that was too dark and hurtful to contemplate for long.

In the firelight her body appeared bathed in gold, but beneath his hands, he could feel how chill she was. Swiftly, he bent and took hold of the afghan on the couch, wrapping it around her.

As quickly, he lifted her. The cabin's bathroom was his single great indulgence, an admission that for all the rigorous discipline of his life he was still an innately sensual man.

Paneled in knotted pine, lit by skylights, the room was warmed by a wood stove set across from the large, black onyx tub. Gently, he set Nickie down on a stool and opened the faucets. Steam rose as the tub began to fill.

While he waited, he lifted her and carefully unwound the afghan. The bruise on her forehead was more evident now. It stood out starkly against her pale skin. There were shadows beneath her eyes and in the finally drawn hollows of her ribs.

She trembled when he removed the afghan, but made no attempt to resist him. His hands slid down her back, moving beneath the fragile lace and silk of her panties. He eased that last garment from her, then turned with her in his arms and laid her gently in the tub.

Nickie gasped softly as the heated water received her. She stiffened and tried to sit up.

"Easy," Conor murmured. "Just relax. You'll feel better soon."

She said nothing, but her eyes were dark with questions. He had them, too. Where they went from here. Whether the past could truly be put aside. If either of them was capable of the trust and commitment they both so badly needed.

But all that would have to wait. Nothing mattered at that moment except that he know—really know—that she was safe.

Slowly, his hands moved over her, squeezing water from a large sponge. Droplets slid down her breasts, over the taut nipples, along her flat abdomen. Again and again, he squeezed, bathing her with infinite gentleness as the steam continued to rise and the storm raged, without and within.

At last her body glowed, flushed with heat. She stirred under his hands, a softly protesting sound rising in her. Slender fingers touched his shirt.

"You got wet, too," she murmured.

Rain had soaked him but he hardly noticed. The delightful woman reclining in the tub made coherent thought impossible. What Nickie did next did not improve matters.

She rose slightly and turned so that she knelt facing him. Her slim arms lifted, her hands stroking the breadth of his chest beneath the denim work shirt he wore. A small smile played across her mouth as she undid first one button, then another and another.

He put a hand on hers, intending to stop her. "Nickie, I don't think—"

"Good," she murmured. "Thinking can be overdone." She looked at him solemnly. "I know, I've done far too much of it."

Before he could protest further, she released the last button and swiftly parted the sides of his shirt. Her hands—wet and hot from the water—slid along the contoured muscles of his torso.

"You are so beautiful," she murmured, and leaned forward, her lips touching him lightly.

Conor groaned. His head fell back, his eyes tightly closed. He couldn't stand this. He would die from it.

A moment later, he thought he had. Her mouth followed where her hands had been, unabashedly delighting in him. She made a small, female sound deep in her throat and rose further so that her breasts rubbed against the soft hair covering his chest.

A harsh cry broke from him. All his good intentions went flying out into the turbulent night. Swiftly, he gathered her to him, one big hand palming her bottom as the other tangled in her hair, holding her still for the driving hunger of his kiss.

He did not wait but thrust deeply with his tongue, tasting her fully, penetration alternating with withdrawal as he teased them both to a fever pitch.

Water sloshed from the tub but neither noticed. The storm surged in intensity, but again, it meant nothing to the pair so intimately entwined.

Yet, all too soon, their closeness was not enough. Conor hesitated only fractionally. Join her in the tub—a pursuit that might be enjoyable at another time when he could take things more slowly?—or lift her out, lay her on the floor, and satisfy them both then and there?

The floor seemed by far the better alternative and yet there was something indisputably unchivalrous about it. That such a thought even occurred to him was more eloquent proof of his true feelings than he necessarily wanted to acknowledge.

Instead, he took it as a point of honor that he not be so reduced to a state of mindless passion as to lose all consideration for her comfort.

In an exercise of self-discipline that would later—upon reflection—leave him astounded, he stood up and swiftly disposed of his remaining clothes.

Nickie knelt before him, watching with unabashed fascination as he unsnapped his jeans and pulled the zipper down. The rasping sound it made seemed momentarily louder than the wind itself.

As he stared at her, her nipples hardened further, turning from pale to dark rose. She stood, water sliding off her, and stepped gracefully from the tub.

"Let me help."

"No," he said harshly, knowing that if she touched him now, he would be lost.

Her smile deepened, becoming infinitely female. With mock demureness, she waited, her eyes never leaving him as he finished the job of undressing with inelegant haste. All the while, her gaze moved over him slowly, missing nothing.

She touched the tip of her tongue to her upper lip and took a deep breath. Her hands rested lightly on his powerfully muscled shoulders as though to steady herself.

She took a tiny step, another, her lower body touching his. He felt the dampness and heat at the entrance to her womanhood. A pulse leapt in his jaw.

Far in the back of his mind, he was still capable of regret that he'd never thought to carpet the bathroom floor. Thankfully, there were alternatives nearby.

He lifted her boldly, wrapping her legs around his sinewy hips, his hands clasping her buttocks, and walked out of the bathroom. Near the fireplace, he knelt, still holding her, and laid her on the thick carpet.

Swiftly, he came down above her, his lean, powerful thighs straddling her body. He put his hands entirely over her breasts, kneading gently, the callused palms abrading her lightly.

She whimpered and tried to reach for him, but he would not allow it. Instead he began to kiss her, thoroughly and extensively, not merely her mouth but down the length of her body, over every enthralling, intimate, honeyed inch until she was writhing under him, as lost to passion as he was himself.

Her hips arched, her legs falling farther apart. He rose above her, his eyes dark, his burnished features rigid with the force of his need. His hand moved between her silken thighs, touching and stroking. Heat rose, engulfing them both.

He withdrew his hand and thrust deeply. Sinking into the depths of her, he felt a sense of welcome more profound than he had ever known.

Hard upon it came release so intense as to shatter reason. Outside the storm raged. But it was inside that the world trembled.

Chapter 23

Nickie stirred, a slight frown creasing her brow. Slowly, she climbed upward out of a dream so intense that even in the half state between sleep and wakefulness, embarrassment coursed through her.

She couldn't remember exactly what she had dreamed, but it had been incredibly sensual, something about Conor and the storm, him coming to get her and—

Her eyes flickered open. She stared into the glowing red embers of the fire. Instantly a host of sensations crashed through her.

She was lying on her side on a surface that was hard but not uncomfortably so, cushioned by some sort of carpet. It was quieter than she sensed it had been, but the storm still continued.

She was naked, yet she wasn't cold; for close against her, warm and hard and strong, was an unmistakably male body that held her with stark possessiveness.

Conor.

His arm was thrown over her waist, his thigh lay across hers. She could feel his manhood against her buttocks. One hand held her breast. The other rested lightly in her hair.

She was engulfed by him, held captive, unable to move and curiously unwilling even to summon the strength to try.

The details of the night before grew clearer in her mind. Her cheeks warmed for reasons that had nothing to do with the lingering heat of the fire. She had always been unbridled in her response to him but there had never been anything such as this. He took her completely out of herself, made her forget every caution, and released passions in her that she had no idea how to deal with.

A tremor ran through her. She had been incredibly foolish to go out into the storm. Had it also been a terrible mistake to return to the island?

She moved tentatively, trying to free herself from Conor's hold. He murmured in his sleep and tightened his arm around her, as though refusing to let her go.

With a small sigh, she gave up and relaxed against him. In time, she slept again.

And woke to the gentle patter of rain against the windows and the soft whisper of the wind around the cabin. Better rested than she had been in a very long time, despite the night spent on the floor, Nickie smiled. She stretched luxuriantly.

At the sound of a deep, male chuckle, her eyes opened wide. Conor was sitting on the floor beside her. He had on a pair of jeans but nothing else. His hair was rumpled, a night's growth of beard darkened his jaw. He looked almost indescribably gorgeous.

She glanced down quickly, relieved to find that he had covered her with the afghan. It was slight armor against the barrage of sensations he unleashed, but she was glad of it all the same.

"Good morning," he said, still looking at her. His voice was low and caressing, tinged with lazy humor and pure male contentment. He reminded her of a very large, powerful cat basking in the sun after having hunted well.

Primal feminine resentment stirred in her, but only weakly. She was too honest to deny that their mating of the night before had been anything other than an encounter of equals.

"Good morning," she replied softly with an edge of tentativeness.

His smile deepened. "Sleep well?"

She straightened up, leaning on her elbows. "Tolerably. You?"

"Not bad. It's still blowing outside but it's not as bad as it was."

"That's good."

They stared at each other, eyes searching, weighted with questions neither was prepared to give voice to just then.

"Hungry?" Conor asked.

In fact, she was ravenous. At her quick nod, he handed her an oversize plaid shirt of soft wool in muted colors of blue and green. Oversize for her, that was, since it clearly belonged to him.

She put it on quickly, holding the afghan in front of her until she was safely covered. Such modesty at this point seemed ridiculous, but she felt so achingly vulnerable.

Wrapped in the shirt, which came almost to her knees, she followed him into the kitchen.

"The power's out," he said. "But that's to be expected."

She nodded, remembering all the times they'd gone without power when she was a kid. It was actually a lot better these days with far more of the electrical lines buried underground. All the same, it would be a while before full power was restored.

"Fortunately," Conor added, "I've got a gas stove."

"Let me help," she said as he took eggs and other supplies from the refrigerator, closing it again quickly to retain the cold. "I actually make pretty good French toast."

"French toast it is," he said. His hand brushed hers as he passed over the carton of eggs. They worked in silence. He heated water and poured it into a drip

coffeepot, mixed frozen orange juice, and warmed
maple syrup in a small pan.

Nickie busied herself with the French toast, mixing
eggs and milk seasoned with cinnamon she found in a
rack over the window. The whisk she used was one of
three of varying sizes. There was a similar choice of
frying pans and spatulas. It was a well-equipped
kitchen, well suited to a man who was unabashedly
self-sufficient.

When the food was ready, they took it back into the
living room. Conor poked up the fire. Outside the sky
remained leaden. It would be hours yet before anyone
stirred on the island and even then there'd be few
places to go. The ferry wouldn't be running for at least
another day, the airport would be shut down and no
boats would be going out.

Deep inside, Nickie admitted that she didn't mind
their isolation. The storm held the rest of the world at
bay, giving them an interlude entirely their own.

What they made of it was strictly up to them.

"Coffee?" Conor asked.

"Please." She held her cup out.

"More syrup?"

"That's fine, thank you."

It was all so polite, as though they were engaged in
the steps of a very formal dance, coming closer, re-
treating, touching, not touching, and all the while a
very different, more primitive rhythm played within
them.

Conor smiled as he leaned back against the pillows they had heaped in front of the fire. He held out a forkful of the French toast. "You first."

She hesitated, but only for an instant. Hunger got the better of her, not for the first time. Leaning forward, she parted her lips slightly and let him slip the tempting morsel into her mouth.

He laughed at her unfeigned enjoyment and fed her again. She reciprocated. They passed forkfuls back and forth. Inevitably the syrup dripped. Droplets of it fell onto his bare chest. He made to wipe it away with a napkin but Nickie forestalled him.

"Let me," she murmured, and touched her mouth to his skin, licking him delicately.

He groaned, the muscles in his throat working. Emboldened, she went further, making a thorough job of it. His skin was smooth and hard, like velvet laid over granite. He smelled of soap and wood smoke, the sweet fading tang of maple mingling with an intrinsically male scent.

She raised her head and with her fingertips alone, stroked him with feather-soft touches, tracing the contours of powerful muscles developed through years of hard, relentless exertion. There was a wild quality of untamed places and majestic forces brought together in this man, here beneath her hands. It excited her tremendously.

Conor stood her love play as long as he could, but where she was concerned, his self-control was never more than tenuous. When her teeth closed with delicious lightness around his flat male nipple, he gave up all restraint and reached for her.

His hands reached up under the soft plaid shirt, stroking her from thigh to throat. Gently, he kneaded her breasts, caressing the full undercurve. She moaned softly and arched her back, silken hair tumbling over her shoulders.

She was all fire and heat, feminine grace and strength, hunger and satisfaction wrapped up in one.

And she was his.

A fierce possessiveness took hold in him, growing with every instant. It wasn't modern, it wasn't fashionable, and heaven knew it wasn't politically correct. But he wanted this woman utterly, wanted to know her in every possible way, to take her so completely that where one of them ended and the other began became a question.

Swiftly, he moved to remove his jeans. But again, as she had before, she stopped him. Her eyes were smoky, her breasts heavy in his hands. She moved against him restlessly.

"Please," Nickie whispered huskily, "no time..."

He felt the tremors coursing through her, through him, and knew she was right. Without restraint, the wildness seizing him, he spread his arms beneath the shirt and simply ripped the buttons off. His dark head lowered, his mouth closing on her nipple, and he suckled her urgently.

She cried out and reached for the zipper of his jeans, undoing it with near-frantic haste. He sprang, hard and long, into her hand. They fell across the couch,

Conor on his back, Nickie rising above him. She tossed the golden mane of her hair as she straddled him and swiftly, without hesitation, drew him into her.

French toast. He'd never thought of it as an aphrodisiac but obviously he'd have to reconsider. She was hot and wet, incredibly tight and fully ready for him.

Loving her, adoring her body and soul, he rammed his hips upward, driving into her. His hands on her satiny bottom, he lifted her once, twice, again. She took the rhythm as she took him, making it her own, making him hers.

Soft pleasure sounds broke from her. Her head fell back, the delicate blue tracings on veins in her throat pulsed lightly. Slim, restless hands fluttered over his chest.

He raised himself enough to take the dark crest of her breast into his mouth. His tongue and teeth teased her and his hand slid down to where they were joined, finding her most sensitive flesh and stroking it lightly.

The orgasmic scream that tore from her shattered the silence of the cabin and challenged the lingering power of the storm. Conor made an exultant sound of male triumph even as he surrendered to her.

Chapter 24

To his people, he was a mighty chieftain. To his enemies, he was a warrior to be feared. But to the woman who stood before him, proudly naked in the flickering firelight, he was the man she meant to make her own. No matter how great the risk. Boldly, she stepped toward him.

Conor smiled lazily as he flipped through the book. He was standing in the kitchen, absently sipping a cup of coffee and waiting for Nickie to finish dressing.

It was midafternoon. The storm was over but the lingering aftereffects remained. The power was still out and it was very quiet over the island.

After breakfast, and what had followed, they had napped. But now the day beckoned.

"Ready?" Nickie asked. She stood in the kitchen door, wearing the slacks she'd had on the previous day

but in one of his sweaters, her own still being too wet
to wear. The sweater was ridiculously big on her, she
could have used it as a dress.

He smiled as his eyes swept over her. Her face was
without makeup and she had left her hair loose. She
looked endearingly lovely.

His body stirred. He shook his head in amazement.

"What's wrong?" she asked.

"Nothing," he said, and quickly slipped the book
out of sight. "Let's take that walk."

The fresh scent of a world washed clean struck them
the moment they opened the door. It was instantly in-
vigorating.

Conor took a quick look to confirm that the Jeep
had come through unscathed. Numerous twigs and
small branches were down, but the majestic pines that
skirted the edge of the cabin remained intact.

The path down to the beach was obscured by debris but they were able to follow it slowly. Conor had
moved his racing shell inside and left the Boston
whaler to ride out the storm at what he'd hoped would
be a safe distance from shore.

Once again, his luck had held. From where he stood
at the end of the path, he could see the vessel undamaged, bobbing up and down on the waves.

Of the beach itself, only a narrow strip remained.
Conor took Nickie's hand. They walked carefully.

"Tide's turning," he said. "This should be the
worst of it."

"Thank heaven for that. I didn't realize it would be
this bad."

He nodded. Automatically, his gaze scanned the beach, assessing the damage.

All things considered, they'd gotten off lightly, at least on this part of the island. The worst of the storm seemed to have struck the other side.

"We'll have lost another piece along the bluffs," he said. "Sooner or later, the whole thing's going to give way."

For a moment, he thought of the houses Ed had built. The storm hadn't been bad enough to put them in any immediate danger, but their eventual fate had to be increasingly clear, if only to the developer himself. It would be one more source of pressure on him.

"What are you thinking about?" Nickie asked.

"Nothing," he lied without compunction. The day was too glorious to waste on Ed. Until life on the island started up again, he was free to concentrate strictly on Nickie and that was exactly what he intended to do.

Seabirds circled overhead as they walked along the beach. Her hand was in his, his step shortened to match hers. Contented silence flowed between them. Until she spotted something up ahead.

"Oh, look," she said, letting go of his hand to run ahead, stopping in front of a small rock pool. Gracefully, she bent and picked up a glistening shell.

"It's unbroken," she said as she brought it back to him.

He turned it over in his hands, examining the perfect symmetry of the twisting spiral. The shell had belonged to a departed conch, a creature of wonder who decorated the inside of his abode with glistening peach and blue inlay and set it to music with the sound of the sea.

"Isn't it beautiful?" she asked.

"Beautiful," he agreed, looking at her. She had a child's excitement, as though this was the first shell ever on the first beach ever at the very dawn of the world.

It was contagious. He laughed and gently set the shell down on a nearby rock, to be retrieved later. "Let's see what else we can find," he said, and took her hand again.

Where the beach curved out in a small promontory, the going got tougher. They had to step carefully to avoid the innumerable small rocks that littered the sand.

The sun was bright, the sky azure blue dotted by a last few scudding clouds. The water dazzled, the air enticed. The day was a feast spread out for their enjoyment.

"When I was a kid," Conor said quietly, "I loved storms. I used to go sit in the cupola on top of the house where I could see them coming from all directions."

She thought of him there, alone in his aerie, and smiled. "I never thought of you doing anything like that. You were always surrounded by friends, always playing football or captaining the debating team. All that stuff."

He winced and looked apologetic. "Is that really how I came across? A combination jock nerd?"

Her eyes danced with laughter. "Hey, you were a terribly impressive older man. All the girls talked about you."

Despite himself, he was curious. Those days seemed so long ago and so much had happened since. It was a part of the time when their lives had touched each other that he felt he hardly knew.

"Did you, listen I mean?"

"You bet."

"What did they say?"

"Terrible things. You wouldn't want to know."

"Oh, yeah, that's what you think. Tell me."

She shook her head, skipping away from him. The oversize sweater hid the slender contours of her body but it didn't matter. He knew every inch of her now, knew the little sounds she made in the heat of passion, the exact spot in her throat where a pulse beat, the lilac-tinged scent of her skin, the silken flesh and heated warmth—all were etched into his very soul.

His body stirred. He shut his eyes for a moment in mingled astonishment and exasperation. He might as well be eighteen again. Perhaps where she was concerned, he always would be.

When he opened his eyes again she was looking at him. The expression on her face was a delicate balance between desire and hesitation.

He mustered a smile. "Terrible things?"

She laughed. "Your head's big enough."

So was something else, but he didn't choose to dwell on that. "I'll have you know I was strictly a gentleman."

"Like I said, terrible." Her eyes rolled in mock dismay. "The disappointment, the teeth gnashing, the anguish."

Despite himself, he laughed. "Surely, it wasn't that bad?"

"Are you kidding? There were days when you were the sole topic in the girl's locker room."

Dryly he said, "My illusions are shattered. I thought the fair sex was the last bastion of decorum."

"Then you just weren't paying attention. What was that blonde's name, the one who always wore red nail polish?"

"I forget."

"Liar. She sat next to you in every class she could. She even signed up for physics when you did."

He sighed. "Amanda. Amanda Dickerson."

"That was her. You dated her."

"Twice."

"What made you stop?"

"I feared for my virtue."

"I'm serious."

Conor stopped. They had come to another curve in the beach. He recognized the place and knew what lay ahead, but he suspected Nickie didn't.

His hand brushed her arm, drawing her to him. He cupped her face lightly and looked down into her eyes. "So am I."

She stiffened and her playful manner vanished. On a breath of sound, she murmured, "You really are."

The corners of his mouth lifted. "Didn't you suspect, that first time?"

Her gaze filled with wonder. Softly she said, "A little, but I was never sure of...of anything."

"And now?" He was very still inside, waiting for what she would say. Hoping.

Her smile when it came was dazzling. "And now," she said, "everything is different."

Chapter 25

They sat on the boulders tumbled at the bottom of the cliff. Water danced in the small pools caught between them. Nickie was very quiet. She had her knees drawn up to her chin and was staring off into space.

"Penny," Conor said softly.

She turned to look at him. Her eyes were sad. "I'm thinking I was a fool."

He didn't have to ask what she meant, here in this place of such intimate memory. But he didn't agree with her, either.

"You were young and scared. So was I."

"At least you weren't afraid to make a commitment. All I wanted was to run off and hide some place. Alone."

"That was hardly surprising given what you'd been through. You'd never had a chance to really trust anyone."

"You didn't exactly have it easy yourself."

"I was still better off than you were. God knows my parents were never the best example of a happily married couple, but they did have moments when they were decent to each other. That let me see the possibilities at least."

He was silent for a moment, looking at her. She still appeared deep in the throes of regret.

Quietly he asked, "Why do you write the books you do?"

She glanced up, startled. "What books?"

He smiled very gently. "The ones I've read."

Her eyes widened as the color seeped from her face. "You're kidding, aren't you?"

"'Fraid not. They had them all down at the newsstand. I got a copy of each. By the way," he added playfully, "what does happen to Baron Padraic and his lady?"

"She decides her true calling is as an abbess and leaves him."

"I don't believe you."

Nickie grimaced. "Oh, all right, they live happily ever after. That's what they're supposed to do."

"What's wrong with that?"

"Nothing, in a book. In real life...it's harder."

"Wait a second," he protested. "Your characters seem to go through a hell of a lot before they reach the finish line."

"In a book, Conor. It's a fantasy, that's all."

"They seem real enough when you're reading them. Is writing them so very different?"

"No," she admitted softly. "Sometimes they seem real to me, too."

"Is that why you write them?"

"I suppose, maybe. They make people happy. There's nothing wrong with that."

"I'd be the last person to suggest otherwise. How did you get started?"

"I loved reading them. They were my secret addiction. I also wanted to write. Eventually, I put two and two together and decided to give it a try."

"They're . . . kind of intense in places."

"You mean, the sex?"

"Well, yeah, if you want to put it like that."

She shot him a quick look and grinned. "Why Conor McDonnell, I swear you're blushing."

"Am not."

"Are so. Don't tell me my sweet little books actually embarrassed you?"

His eyebrows rose. "Sweet? Ye gods, woman, you could fry eggs on them."

She chortled, unabashedly pleased. "Do you really think so?"

He shot her a long, hard look. "Let's just say you've got a hell of an imagination." There was a pause of the sort usually called pregnant. "Right?"

She got the message loud and clear. Laughing, she rose and went to him. He drew her between his long legs, holding her.

Her fingers caressed his cheek. He'd shaved that morning. The chiselled line of his jaw was smooth. She thought of how it had felt against her in the night, roughly abrading, and felt a tiny dart of regret.

"You are a wonderful man," she said, her lips brushing his.

"Hmm."

"And a memorable one."

"Oh?"

"Extremely memorable. Even, you might say, inspirational."

"I'm flattered." He was, immensely, but modesty forbade him from going on about it. .

Again, her lips touched his. The effect was predictable. His big hands closed around her, drawing her into the circle of his embrace. His kiss was hard, hot and hungry. Gone was the slightly clumsy ardor of youth. In its place was raw male need and determination.

"It's a shame it isn't summer," he said thickly against her throat, thinking of how very easy it would be to lay her down on the smooth sand in the shadow of the boulders and find again the ecstasy they had first discovered there.

She nodded, her heart pounding with his. "A summer night."

He raised his head, a smile dancing around his mouth. "Fortunately, I can suggest an alternative."

"The back of a '78 Chevy?"

He looked at her in pretended shock. "Control yourself, woman. Obviously, you're prey to wicked thoughts of the decadent variety. We'll have to do something about that."

"Promise?"

"Oh, yes," he said, and meant it.

The return walk along the beach was quicker. They did not stop to admire the view or contemplate the results of the storm.

But they did remember to pick up the undamaged shell Nickie had found. It sat on the bedside table, silent witness to a love deep and wild as the sea it had come from.

Toward evening, they slept, wrapped around each other, and did not wake. Not even when the lights flicked on again and slowly, but inexorably, the life of the island resumed.

"Do you have to?" Nickie asked. The question was wrenched from her. She knew she sounded clinging and demanding, but she couldn't seem to help it.

Conor nodded reluctantly. They had just finished breakfast. Outside the day was crystal-clear. Except for the debris that still littered the ground, all signs of the storm had vanished.

"I really do. Ed's got to be brought to heel fast before anything more happens."

"You're sure he's responsible?"

"Not entirely. There's one or two things that don't add up but—"

"But what?"

"It's not important. What matters is that this isn't the safest place to be at the moment. Ed knows that

I'm suspicious of him and he just might do something foolish."

Nickie's eyes widened. "How does he know that?"

Conor sighed, wishing he didn't have to tell her. But she deserved the truth. "Because I told him."

"You *what?*"

"It's an old trick," he insisted. "Make the guy sweat so he does something stupid and screws up. We use it all the time." Actually, that wasn't entirely correct. It was more of a desperation ploy and he'd definitely jumped the gun resorting to it so quickly. But he wanted this tied up nice and fast so that he could concentrate on Nickie.

Not that he was about to tell her that. "It's S.O.P.," he said. "Standard operating procedure."

"How enlightening. Here I was thinking you were a U.S. Marshal when in fact you're Grade A Bait."

Give her top marks for being clearheaded, Conor thought. That just about nailed his job description, at least for the moment.

"It's going to be fine," he said. "Or it will be if you'll just do as I ask."

"What's that?"

"Go back to Connecticut." It was only four small words, but she was shaking her head before he got the last one out.

Quickly he added, "Just for a few days. I'll be able to wrap this up a whole lot faster if I don't have to worry about you at the same time."

"Then don't."

"Easier said than done. Ed's seen us together. He just might get it into his head to come after you instead of me." He spoke calmly enough, but the possibility filled him with gut-twisting dread. She had to see things his way.

Nickie hesitated. She clearly didn't like what she was hearing but at least she was listening.

"Look," he said, "we both love the island, but wouldn't you like to have some time away from here? Just the two of us without Dan and Donna and Mabel and Georgina and all the rest? How about it?"

"Sounds great but..."

"No buts. I've been on this case and others just like it for a solid three years. With Ed, there's a chance I can wrap it up once and for all. But not if I have to worry about you at the same time."

"You don't realize how hard it is to—"

"Yes," he said softly, his finger stroking her cheek. "I do. I know how I'd feel if our positions were reversed. But believe me, this is for the best."

She grimaced. "I haven't said I'll go."

"You will," he promised, and set about convincing her in the most persuasive way possible.

Chapter 26

The cabin seemed cold and empty after Nickie's departure. Conor had driven her back to Gull's Rest and waited while she got her things together. He'd waited again while she'd caught the ferry, not leaving until it pulled out from the dock and had started toward the mainland.

She'd said little. There was a quick, fierce embrace, a kiss that was almost chaste, and a single, murmured "Call me." Then she was gone.

He would, he promised himself. First, tonight to make absolutely sure that she was home safe. Again in the morning if he could possibly manage it. He needed the sound of her voice, needed to know that she existed, that she was real. That she was his.

But before all that, he had to deal with Ed. Except for a few workmen cleaning up around the premises, there was no sign of activity at Mulloney Development. The house out on the bluffs also appeared deserted.

Not so at the Clamshell. In the aftermath of the storm, people had a natural inclination to gather together. They were choosing to do so over coffee and pancakes.

Ed was at a table near the door. He had a plate in front of him, but he was looking up as Conor came in. For an instant, he seemed to hesitate. "Join me?"

Conor was surprised. He wasn't used to Ed being cordial. The hairs at the back of his neck went up. Taking due note of that, he nodded. "Sure, why not?"

The two men settled across from each other with the table between them. They exchanged a cautious glance.

"Come through the storm okay?" Ed asked.

"Pretty much. You?"

"I guess." Ed still looked doubtful. Conor wondered if that was because of the condition of the bluffs or if it was something unrelated.

Norm ambled over to take his order. Conor wasn't particularly hungry, but he allowed as to how coffee and a bagel sounded good. Ed took a refill on the coffee and another blueberry muffin. Conor noted in passing that he wasn't drinking.

The food came. They ate with little conversation except for a few comments on the general unreliability of weather forecasts these days and the outlook for a tough winter.

When he was done Ed pushed his plate away, stuck a toothpick in his mouth, and said, "Guess I should thank you for the other day."

Conor shrugged. "It isn't necessary."

"If you say so." His brows drew together. "Booze hit me harder than usual."

"It has a way of doing that, especially as you get older."

Ed laughed humorlessly. "Ain't it the truth? Nothing's as good as it was when we were kids."

Conor didn't agree but he saw no reason to say so. Ed was leading up to something. It was better to let him get there his own way.

Minutes ticked past. A stranger coming upon the scene might have taken the two men sharing a table for old friends who didn't need a whole lot of conversation. Only someone who knew them could have sensed the tension.

Finally Ed asked, "You still on that dumping thing?"

Conor's expression didn't change. Inwardly he felt a sudden rush of excitement as when the quarry is sighted. But he was also intrinsically cautious. "Sure am."

"You realize some not-nice people could be mixed up in it?"

"It happens."

Ed shook his head. "I don't get you. What do you need this kind of aggravation for?"

"You want the twenty-dollar speech on the importance of protecting the environment?"

"Hell, no."

"Okay. This amounts to dumping garbage in my front yard and I don't like it. End of story."

"Jeez, I'd hate to see how you get about something actually important."

Again Ed fell silent and again Conor let him. He used the time to assess the other man, trying to sense what was going on inside him.

On the one hand, Ed seemed sincerely appreciative of the help Conor had given him and inclined, because of that, to open up about the dumping.

On the other, the whole thing might be a sham.

"You understand," Ed said, keeping his voice low, "I've got to be careful?"

"Don't we all?"

"Yeah, well, it's my hide I'm thinking of. You got to promise to keep me out of it."

Keeping his face blank, Conor said, "If I can, I will." He would pledge nothing more. Indeed, he could not.

Ed looked doubtful, as though he'd wanted more. But after a moment, he nodded. "Give me a couple of minutes, then follow me out. We'll swing by the office."

He stood up, nodded again, and went over to the counter to settle up with Norm. Conor waited.

When the door had swung shut behind Ed, he sat, sipping his coffee, silently counting. Two minutes later, he got up, tossed a bill on the table, and left.

Ed's Caddy was already gone, but he'd expected that. He drove slowly, careful of the downed trees and other debris that littered the road.

The workmen were gone from around the development company's office. Ed's car wasn't in sight but a quick drive-around revealed that he'd parked in back. Conor did the same.

He sat for a moment, considering one last time if he really wanted to do this. The manual called for backup and he had called in a status report to the home office before the storm hit. The question was, could he afford to wait for a response?

All the signs Ed was giving off indicated that he was about to crack. But in another day or two—hell, in another hour—he might think better of it. If Conor waited, the opportunity could be lost.

Nobody paid him *not* to take chances. Or as he preferred to put it, prudent risks.

His mind made up, he got out of the Jeep and climbed the stairs to the front door. It was open. Inside, the long hallway lined with desks and cubicles was empty. It was a Saturday, but even if it hadn't been, everyone was too busy cleaning up from the storm to be expected to work.

There was a light on in the office at the far corner. Ed was standing at the desk in front of a computer monitor that was on. His cheeks were slightly flushed and he was frowning.

"Come on in."

Conor walked across the room and joined Ed at the desk. He glanced at the monitor. The screen was covered with neatly ordered words and numbers. "What's this?"

"Records, inventories, receipts. You name it."

"For what?"

"You know what. Here, take a look."

Still, Conor hesitated. He remained upright, watching Ed. "You keep all this stuff written down?"

"Why not? I like to know what's what. Besides, you could say I wanted a little leverage."

It made sense. Ed was far from stupid. If he wasn't running the dumping business on his own—and Conor had never thought that he was—then he'd naturally need some protection against business associates who tended to settle their disputes out of court. Far out.

Slowly, Conor slid into the chair. He was still alert to the possibility of trouble, but the words on the screen distracted him. He recognized the name of a mainland business he knew, and another. Quickly he scanned the list, then went back and started reading more carefully.

The file was a gold mine—names, dates, numbers. It was all there, socked away in the belly of Ed's computer. Enough sheer data to blow the lid off what had to be the biggest illegal dumping scheme in the northeast.

Whoo-ee.

"Looks like you've been busy," he said, still studying the screen.

"Yeah," Ed replied. "Had to be once the construction dried up."

"Pretty tricky dealing with boys this big."

"I went where the money was, that's all. But you see now who they are, why I gotta protect myself."

"Yeah, I see—"

"Including against you, buddy. Kind of a shame you fell for it."

Conor was almost blindingly fast, out of the chair and turning, hand going to the holster at the small of his back, all in one fluid motion. But it wasn't enough.

Ed was prepared, had known exactly what he'd do from the moment Conor had walked into the café. He'd seen his chance and he'd taken it.

He, too, was armed.

Conor's next-to-last thought was that another second—a bare instant—and it would have been okay.

Instead, it wasn't.

His actual last thought was a single word pent up with all the longing and regret of his life:

Nickie.

Chapter 27

The woman ahead of her had a small child half
asleep on her shoulder and two oversize bags. Nickie
helped her down the stairs and carried the bags to her
car. The thanks she received suggested such help was
regretfully rare.

That small Samaritan act meant that she was the last
to drive onto the dock at Point Judith. In summer the
fishing port was always busy with visitors going to and
from the island, but at this time of year, it was quiet.

Nickie swung out onto the main road and was preparing to make the left turn that would eventually take
her to the highway when she hesitated. On the ride
over the regret she'd felt at leaving Conor had been
eased by the conviction that she was doing the right
thing. Without her there, he'd be better able to con-

centrate on his work. He'd get it done and then come to Connecticut. They'd be together again soon.

But now, sitting behind the wheel, she hesitated. She couldn't explain what she was feeling—not even to herself—but a queer sort of unease seemed to have seized her. And it was different from the ordinary sort of worry any woman would be bound to feel for a man she cared about who was potentially going into danger.

Very different.

Her skin felt strange, as though it no longer quite fit her. Her hands were cold and a deep hollow had opened up in her stomach. Even her vision suddenly seemed blurred.

She blinked once, twice, trying to clear it. Maybe she was coming down with something. But she seemed healthy enough, only in the grip of a sensation she had never experienced before.

A horn blared behind her. Abruptly she realized that she was blocking a pickup. The logical thing to do was drive ahead, go home, wait for Conor. Exactly as they'd planned.

Instead she pulled over to the side and let the pickup pass. Parked at the curb, she sat and tried to think sensibly.

There wouldn't be another ferry for a couple of hours. It was absolutely ridiculous for her to sit here all that time, worrying. Besides, what would Conor think if she suddenly showed up again?

It would look as though she didn't trust him to take care of the matter on his own. And as though she couldn't keep her word.

A classic, no-win situation.

Be smart, her brain said. Head for home and wait. He'll be there soon.

Be careful, her heart said. This hurts and we've been through enough already.

Be wise, her soul murmured, far down in the deep reaches of her being. Be ...

Be what? Serious about some vague sensation she couldn't explain or identify? Risk a relationship that was just beginning to have a chance on what might turn out to be a garden-variety virus?

She'd run before.

This wasn't running. They'd talked it over together and decided she should go.

Then. This was now.

Nothing had changed.

Yes, it had. She could feel it.

Trust, said her soul, so softly she could hardly hear. But then she wasn't really used to listening to that part of her. Few people were.

Trust him. Go home.

Trust your instincts. Go back.

There was a phone by the ferry office. Nickie punched in a series of numbers and waited. Five rings ... six. There was no answer at the cabin.

Okay, he'd gone off somewhere. She'd try the Clamshell, claim she'd forgotten something and needed to get in touch with Conor.

"He left a while ago," Norm said. "Had breakfast with Ed and took off."

"With who?"

"Ed Mulloney. Want to leave a message?"

"No...I don't think so. You say you haven't seen him since?"

"Nope, can't say I have. Where are you calling from, Miss Chandler?"

"The dock at Point Judith. I'm heading back to Connecticut for a while."

"That's fine, then," Norm said. "When I see McDonnell, I'll be sure and say you called."

"Thanks, I appreciate that."

"Don't mention it."

She hung up and stood for a moment, staring at the phone. The feeling she'd had was stronger than ever.

Slowly she walked back to her car.

A symphony of sledgehammers played in Conor's head. He groaned and squeezed his eyes shut, wishing he could do the same with his ears.

Not that it would have helped. His head felt as though it was about to split open from the inside out. He groaned again and gingerly felt his scalp.

His fingers came away sticky. Ed's bullet had grazed him at the hairline.

Either the guy had been more nervous than he looked or he was a really lousy shot. A quarter inch the other way and waking up wouldn't have been a problem. Or a possibility.

Slowly, using every ounce of willpower he possessed, he forced himself to move. As he lifted his head from the rough wooden floor, a wave of dizziness washed over him, so intense that he feared he would lose consciousness again. But the worst of it passed and he was finally able to push himself into a sitting position.

Through the cracks in the wall next to him, he could catch glimpses of daylight. His watch showed he'd been out just over an hour.

He had to give Ed credit, he'd done a real thorough job. But of what, exactly?

He'd been shot and then dumped somewhere. That much was obvious, but not a whole lot else. For instance, how was all this supposed to help Ed?

He shut his eyes. When he opened them, they were better adjusted to the darkness. He was in a small room, little bigger than a shed. Crates with stenciled lettering were stacked around him.

Curious, he dragged himself upright and peered closer to get a look at the stenciling.

A second later, he almost regretted doing so. The message was short and to the point. TNT.

Well, that certainly cleared up the mystery of what old Ed had in mind. Tempting though it was to think the shed just happened to be a convenient place to stash him, he had to believe otherwise.

What better way to get rid of the proverbial thorn in the side? Blow him to kingdom come and then look as shocked as everybody else. There wouldn't be enough left to prove anything one way or another.

Ed would easily claim that Conor had insisted on checking the shed. That he'd asked him to wait until he could be escorted, but that Conor had preferred to go it alone.

People who didn't routinely handle explosives shouldn't be allowed anywhere near them. It was a real shame.

All of which meant there had to be a trigger ticking somewhere. Ed wouldn't want to take any chances. He'd need a nice, guaranteed explosion that would do the job while he himself was well away from the scene.

A quick look around the shed revealed nothing. Wherever the timer was, it wasn't inside. Ed must have wired it up after dropping him on the floor; that left it on the other side of the door when he left.

There were no windows in the shed, the only light came through a few cracks in the walls. The door was metal and heavily bolted.

Grimly, Conor set himself to the task of finding a way out even as he knew that there might well be none.

Chapter 28

There was no sign of life at the cabin. All the lights were off and the door was firmly locked. Conor's Jeep was gone.

Slowly, Nickie parked and got out. There didn't seem much point to going any farther, but just on the off chance that Conor might be there, she decided to knock.

Several loud tries brought no response. Reluctant to give up, and more deeply worried than even before, she peered in a window.

The living room looked just as it had when she'd last seen it. Nothing seemed to have been disturbed. She leaned closer, looking in the direction of the worktable. Were those the water samples Conor had been testing?

A hard hand slammed down on her shoulder, spinning her around and pinning her against the wall of the cabin.

Terror rose in her. She stared into the grim face of a very large, very angry-looking man. Another who might have been his fraternal twin was right behind him.

Both were wearing gray business suits, white shirts and striped ties. Both had bulges under their jackets that owed nothing to muscles—which they also possessed in abundance—and everything to firearms.

"Who are you?" Nickie demanded. She was very proud of the fact that she sounded merely frightened. The spine-shivering terror she actually felt was well concealed.

The first man, the one who had grabbed her, ignored her question. Before she realized what was happening, he ran a hand down her impersonally from her neck to her feet. Straightening, he said, "She's clean, Dave."

Nickie swallowed hard. That terror was getting harder and harder to hide.

"What's your name?" Dave demanded.

Nickie didn't even think about not answering. He had the same quiet sort of authority Conor did. However, that didn't mean she had to like it.

"Nickie Chandler. Who the hell are you?"

"Do you know whoever lives here?" the first man asked.

"Conor McDonnell. I asked who you are."

The men glanced at each other. They looked back at her with frank assessment. Slowly they relaxed. The Dave one even smiled a little.

"Sorry," he said. "Phil and I always figure it's better to be on the safe side."

"Too bad Conor doesn't feel the same."

Phil's eyebrows arched. "Care to explain that?"

"Not until I'm sure who you are."

They had badges in nice leather cases, which they obligingly opened and showed her.

"We're friends of Conor's," Dave said. He looked a little sheepish. "We would have been here sooner, but with the storm and all . . ."

"Conor wouldn't wait."

The two men exchanged a look. "That so?" Phil asked.

"He had breakfast with Ed Mulloney. Does that name mean anything to you?"

"Maybe. Any idea where they are now?"

"None. I was hoping you'd know."

Maybe they did and maybe they didn't. Either way, they weren't saying.

"Why don't you just get some rest, Miss Chandler," Phil suggested. It was the equivalent of a verbal pat on the head. Just as Conor had wanted her off somewhere out of the way, so did they.

"Tell me first what you're going to do," she said.

They hesitated. Finally Dave answered. "Look around, ask a few questions. That's all."

"It's not enough. You should find Ed Mulloney fast and make him tell you where he and Conor went. If you can't find him, you should search his office and his home."

"We could do that," Phil allowed, that simple admission telling her how far this had already gone. "Take a while, though. There *are* formalities."

"Then if I were you," Nickie said succinctly, "I'd get started on them."

As for herself, she wasn't waiting.

Conor cursed under his breath. He was in worse shape than he'd thought. Half an hour or so of trying to break through the wall and already he was feeling winded.

Maybe it had something to do with almost taking a bullet in the brain.

It might be a good idea to sit down and rest for a minute, except that he couldn't be sure it wouldn't be his last.

Gritting his teeth, he backed up, ran and hit the wall again full force. His arm and shoulder screamed in protest but he barely noticed. This time, he thought, though he wasn't completely sure, he'd felt the wall give very slightly. He steeled himself to try yet again.

A car was parked in front of Ed's house. It wasn't the Caddy he drove but a nondescript sedan that looked as though it had seen better days.

When Nickie rang the bell, a short, stern-faced woman answered. "Yes," she said cautiously, "may I help you?"

Nickie smiled, trying her best to look friendly and harmless even though she was feeling anything but.

"I'm looking for Mr. Mulloney. Is he in?"

The woman shook her head. "Haven't seen him. I'm just in to clean. He usually doesn't get back until I've finished and gone."

"I see. This is really very urgent. He was supposed to leave word for me where we were to meet." She lied without compunction. Whatever it took, she was getting inside.

"Do you think there might be something here to tell me where he's gone? A phone number on the refrigerator, a note on the message board, something like that?"

The woman looked doubtful. "Can't say I've noticed anything. But then I've had my hands full."

"Pretty messy?" Nickie asked sympathetically.

"Not usually." She stood aside to let her enter. "Between you and me, this isn't much of a job. Mr. Mulloney's hardly ever here and when he is, it's strictly to sleep. I do the laundry, vacuum—" She eyed Nickie. "Carry out the bottles and that's about it. But this morning—"

"What's the problem?"

The woman shrugged. "I don't know what he was trying to do, cook a big slab of steak, maybe. Or maybe he hurt himself. Anyway, there's blood all over the sink. Makes my skin crawl, it does."

Nickie's throat tightened. It was all she could do to speak normally. "That's a shame. As long as I'm here, why don't I help you clean it up?"

The housekeeper shot her a startled look. "You don't have to do that...."

"It's no trouble. I'll tell you what, I'll clean up the sink and in return you can look around and see if there's any sign of where Mr. Mulloney went."

That satisfied the woman, who wasn't about to question her good luck. She led Nickie into the kitchen and pointed to the sink.

"You sure you don't mind? I'm a vegetarian and I just hate the thought of dealing with that."

"Not at all," Nickie assured her. She was getting good at lies. "Think nothing of it."

Satisfied, the woman went off and a moment later Nickie heard her bustling around in the next room. She walked over to the sink and stared down at it.

There were pale red stains against the porcelain, as though someone had tried to wash up but hadn't managed it very well.

Someone who was in too much of a hurry to do a thorough job.

Or who was perhaps just too scared to notice what he'd left behind.

Sirens sounded off in the distance, but Nickie barely heard them. Nausea filled her. For the first time in years, she prayed.

Chapter 29

If he hit the damned wall again, he was going to pass out.

Slumped in the darkness, fighting for breath, Conor rubbed his bruised and battered shoulder gingerly. The other was in no better shape. As for the rest of him, it didn't bear discussing.

For a moment he wavered. Maybe it was all for nothing. This just might be Ed's idea of a sick joke.

And maybe pigs could fly. He'd misjudged Mulloney once, he wasn't going to do it again. The developer was an extremely frightened man, in over his head in a situation where he couldn't hope to survive.

He was also a drunk, which meant that he was likely to act first and think later. All of which spelled major league trouble.

How long did he have? An hour? Thirty seconds? He couldn't know how much time was left, but it had to be running out fast. Ed wouldn't take a chance on his being found.

There were enough explosives stacked in the shed to make it possible that nobody would ever actually be sure that Conor had gone up with them. He might simply just disappear.

Life was too sweet to let it end that way.

Nickie was too sweet.

Pain enveloped him so completely that when he hit the wall again, he hardly felt it.

"Legally, he was sober," Phil said. "He'd had a couple of drinks but not enough to push him over the limit."

Nickie faced him in the medical center waiting room. She had insisted on coming after running into them at the police station, where she'd been trying to report the bloodstains.

Before she'd gotten two words out, he'd interrupted. Ed Mulloney wasn't missing anymore. He'd just been scraped out of a bad wreck on the road near the boat basin. They were going to have to medevac him to the mainland.

Those had been the sirens she'd heard.

"The cops figure he was doing maybe eighty-five when he came around that curve," Phil went on. "He was in a hell of a hurry to get somewhere."

"The boat yard," Nickie said. "He keeps a cabin cruiser there. He must have been planning to get off the island."

"Maybe. Only one thing doesn't fit."

"What's that?" she asked wearily. God forgive her, but she really didn't care about Ed. He was just a means to try to find Conor.

"It looked like he'd turned around and was heading back toward town."

A nurse appeared at the door to the room. She glanced at Nickie and the two marshals. "Dr. Jefferson can speak with you now."

"Mulloney'll talk," Dave said grimly. "I don't care what the hell condition he's in, we'll open him like a dead clam."

Brave words, Nickie thought, but she privately doubted them. If Ed was in as bad condition as it seemed, they'd never get near him.

When the men had disappeared down the hall, she went over to the nursing station. The woman there was young with wide brown eyes and a gentle smile.

"Excuse me," Nickie said, "were you here when Mr. Mulloney was brought in?"

The nurse nodded. "Are you a relative of his?"

"No, but I'm very concerned about what caused him to have the accident. Did he say any-thing...anything at all?"

"He was deeply unconscious."

"Even so, it seems as though he may have been heading back into town for some purpose. Something he thought was urgent enough to make him go so fast.

If he made any sound, even if it made no sense, I'd appreciate—''

"There *was* something...but it wasn't even a word, exactly."

Nickie's hands were clenched at her sides. She had never had more difficulty controlling herself.

"That's all right. Anything at all."

"Sled," the nurse pronounced. "He said something that sounded like sled." She shrugged apologetically. "But it couldn't have been. It isn't even winter."

Nickie's shoulders sagged. She thanked the nurse and forced herself to walk away. Halfway back to the waiting room, a fleeting thought crossed her mind.

Ed was badly injured, unconscious, possibly dying. Anything he said would have to be hard to understand.

What else sounded like sled?

She was running when she got back to the desk. The nurse looked up, startled.

"Those men who went in to see the doctor," Nickie said, "tell them there's an explosives shed behind Mulloney Development. They've got to get there quick. I'll meet them."

"But, miss..."

"Just tell them," she yelled and was gone.

The pain was so great that he was beginning to hallucinate. Once he thought he saw Nickie, another time he thought he heard her voice. Hell of a way to go, dreaming of the woman he'd hoped to spend the rest of his life with.

Short and sweet, over and done with, until we meet again . . . all that stuff. *Cut it out, McDonnell. Feeling sorry for yourself isn't going to accomplish anything. One more try . . .*

He started to get up again, but this time not even his immense strength was equal to the task. Exhausted, on the verge of unconsciousness, he slumped back down on the floor.

A red mist floated in front of his eyes. There was a dull roar in his ears. Through it, a voice floated, tempting, taunting.

"Conor, are you in there?"

It was happening again. He was imagining that Nickie was near. Fate sure didn't quit. Get a man down, at the end of his run, and torment him a little just for extra.

"Conor, answer me, you've got to be in there."

That was new. Before, the illusion of Nickie had merely whispered sweet enticements. This Nickie sounded scared and angry.

And real.

"Nickie!" Oh, God, no, please don't let her be near. Not here, not now. If he was right and this whole goddamn mess was about to blow . . .

"Nickie, run! Get away from here!"

"Conor, you're alive! Oh, thank God! Hold on, I'm going to get you out. There's a padlock on the door, but . . ."

"Nickie, listen to me! This is a storage shed for dynamite. I think Ed's wired it to blow. Get the hell away."

"Wired it...but..." Stunned, she looked around. The shed looked perfectly ordinary except for—

"Conor, there's something lying out here by the door. It looks like a bundle—"

"Don't touch it, Nickie! Go back to the office and call the police." Pain and exhaustion forgotten, he hauled himself upright, clinging to the wall. "Run, Nickie, right now!"

Leave him? Take the chance that he would still be there when she got back?

In a pig's eye.

"Nickie, what are you doing?"

She didn't answer at once. All her attention was focused on the bundle. Slowly she knelt down in front of it.

"Nickie, listen to me...."

"I am listening. There's what looks like a timer of some kind on this. There are two hands and they're almost together."

"Damn you, run!"

"No!"

He took a deep breath. No time left.

For all the marbles—

For Nickie.

"Is there a red wire connected to what looks like a battery with soft clay packed around it?"

"Yes."

"*Don't touch it.* Find the black wire that runs from there to the timer."

"Got it."

"Pull it."

"Pull...?"

"One good, hard tug." And pray that he was right about how the thing was wired.

Sirens were screaming in the background. The hands on the timer flicked together.

Nickie closed her eyes.

And pulled.

Chapter 30

Outside in the hallway a voice said, "Guess we'll have to wait. Looks like they're pretty busy in there."

"Well, just what did you expect, Donna? 'Course they're busy, they're in love, aren't they?"

Inside, Nickie stirred in Conor's arms. She raised her head and looked toward the door. It was swinging shut again.

He laughed and drew her closer, smoothing her bright hair with a gesture that was at once tender and possessive. Together they listened.

"Told you so," Georgina said. There was no mistaking her satisfaction. "You just can't stand in the path of true love."

"Well, I'm not gonna stand here holding this fruit basket forever," Dan Philips announced. "You all know I've got a bad leg and this thing is going to send my sciatica right into orbit."

"Oh, stop complaining," Mabel ordered. "Put the thing down there. Somebody'll find it and give it to them."

"What's your hurry?" Dan demanded. Nickie wondered the same, but she had a pretty good idea.

"I've got to get dinner on," Mabel said.

"Me, too," Donna said.

"Same here," Georgina declared.

Dan snorted. Steps echoed down the hallway. Half muted, his voice floated back. "Don't see how you're gonna manage it what with calling everybody in creation."

"And why not," Donna called after him. "It's not every day that..."

"Hush, now," Georgina remonstrated. "They'll hear us."

"She's right," Mabel said.

"Come on, we'd better go," Georgina added.

"I guess they'll be opening up the house again," Donna said, more faintly.

"Speaking of which," Mabel said, "did you hear Martha Daniels painted her living room orange?"

"What in creation could she have been thinking of?"

"Well, the way I heard it, she got the idea from—"

"You ought to go home," Conor said, his breath warm against her cheek. He raised his head to look at her.

Under the harsh, fluorescent light of the hospital room, he thought she looked inexpressibly beautiful, but also undeniably exhausted.

"Where's that?" she murmured.

"My place," he said promptly. "I'll give you the key. You can get some rest, take a shower, whatever."

He had no right to look so compellingly masculine stretched out on the hospital bed, his dark hair wreathed in bandages and a sardonic smile playing across his chiseled features. Any minute now one of the nurses who had been fluttering about since the previous day would come in and start making calf's eyes at him again.

Before that happened, maybe she ought to take him up on the offer. She was wrinkled, dirty, and so tired she felt punchy. The mere thought of a hot shower filled her with longing usually reserved for Conor himself.

"Too bad you can't join me," she said huskily.

Conor was going to be fine, but the doctor had really insisted on keeping him overnight. Ed had been medevaced out and the word was he had a decent chance at recovery. Phil and Dave were on their way to the mainland to be there when he started talking.

Nobody doubted that he would. Only the government could provide him with the protection he needed from his erstwhile "associates" and that would come only with his full cooperation.

Besides, Nickie had a strong feeling that having actually come close to killing someone, Ed might just have lost his taste for crime. After all, he had been rushing back into town in what seemed to have been a change of heart.

"Actually," Conor said, "I don't see why I have to stay here. There's nothing wrong with me."

"Nothing but a concussion, two sprained shoulders and enough cuts and bruises for the Super Bowl. You're not going anywhere."

He grumbled, but lay back against the pillows. His face was still pale and she knew he was in pain, having refused most of the medication the doctor had tried to give him. Until she left, he was unlikely to sleep.

"I'm leaving," she said quietly, and stood.

His hand still held hers. She looked down at the long, bronzed fingers lying over her own and smiled.

"You have to let go."

"Never," he murmured, but already his eyes were growing heavy. She slipped her hand from his, bent down and placed a gentle kiss on his mouth.

Silently she slipped from the room.

Outside the medical center, she paused for a moment to fill her lungs with clean, clear air. The sky was awash with stars. A gentle breeze blew from the south.

She drove slowly, in no particular hurry and mindful of how tired she was. The lights were on in the cabin.

She left the car in front, got out and opened the cabin door. Perhaps she'd make a cup of tea before taking that shower. Conor had some decaf in the cupboard, not that it mattered. She could have drunk an ocean of caffeine and still slept.

Tea, definitely. She'd shower while it brewed, curl up in his robe, and find something to read for just a short time. Then to bed and tomorrow—

Tomorrow the doctor said he could probably come home. There would be time alone to talk. To put the past to rest at last and begin looking to the future.

She was nervous about that, but glad, too, excited and happy all at once. It must be the effect of nearly getting blown up, she decided as she went into the kitchen and ran water to fill the kettle.

She was rummaging around in the cabinet when she thought she heard a sound from the living room. But it was gone in an instant and she put it down to the wind.

Leaving the kettle on the counter, she started toward the stairs to the loft. Now where was that robe—

"Hi," Norm said. He stepped out of the shadows near the door, a suddenly tall, menacing figure who took her completely by surprise.

Nickie gave a small scream and backed up quickly. "Norm, what on earth...? What are you doing here?"

And how had he gotten in? She'd locked the door behind her. Hadn't she? Was she so tired that she'd forgotten?

"I heard about Conor," he said. A long sigh escaped him. "Terrible thing."

"Yes, it was." Had he really come by at this time of night to offer his sympathies? Surely that could have waited.

"But he's going to be fine," she assured him. "He just needs a little rest."

Norm nodded gravely. "I heard Ed's going to make it, too."

"It seems so. Well, it was nice of you to stop by but if you'll excuse me, I was just going to—"

"Too bad about that."

"About what?"

"Ed."

"Oh, yes, it's a shame. Apparently he felt too pressured for money, that sort of thing. But at least it seems like he had second thoughts and was trying to save Conor at the end."

Norm's hands were deep in his pockets. His narrow shoulders shrugged. He was looking at her closely.

"You don't say? I always thought Ed was smarter than that."

She must be even more tired than she thought. She could have sworn he'd said— "I'm sorry, I didn't get that."

"No," Norm agreed, "you didn't." He smiled. "But you're going to."

His right hand came out of the pants' pocket. There was a gun in it.

Chapter 31

Conor lay and stared up at the ceiling. He'd drowsed for a few minutes after Nickie had left, but he'd awakened almost immediately and since then he hadn't been able to go back to sleep.

His head throbbed, his shoulders ached and he felt generally lousy. But worst of all, he missed her.

He shouldn't have told her to leave, but he'd had no choice. She was done in and she needed to rest. Tomorrow would come soon enough. They'd have time to talk, to touch, to plan. Time for everything.

He just had to be patient a little while longer. That was why they called them patients, wasn't it? They were supposed to be patient.

He could do that. He had lots of experience waiting things out. It was part of what made him a good investigator.

Thinking of that, he winced. Yeah, real good. He'd walked right into old Ed's trap even though he'd actually known it could be coming. He didn't even have ignorance as an excuse to hide behind.

No doubt about it, his instincts had really let him down. If he'd been just a little less lucky, he would have been dead.

Which made him wonder about his future in the particular end of the business he'd been working in recent years. It wasn't that he was a suspicious man, but he *did* believe there was such a thing as luck. Maybe he'd come to depend too heavily on his.

Maybe it had just about run out.

Nickie was all the luck any man had a right to expect in a lifetime.

There was still a lot to do on the island even once the dumping ring was broken. He could settle down and devote himself to the coastal studies that really were his first love, professionally speaking.

And then there was his other first love.

He smiled as he thought of how she'd looked after she'd let him out, sitting there on the ground in front of the explosives shed with the disconnected black wire in her hand and a most peculiar expression on her face. Almost as though she couldn't decide whether to kiss him or finish what Ed had started.

She'd settled on a kiss, so heated and heartfelt that for a few moments nothing else had mattered. He'd felt on top of the world holding her that way.

Not now, though. Now he felt as though a mountain had fallen on him.

Fat lot of good it was doing lying here.

He shifted slightly in the bed. It hurt but not as much as it had a few hours before. On the second try, he winced but decided to keep going.

Slowly he swung his legs over the side and tried putting his weight on both feet. They held, if only barely.

Feeling pleased with himself, he walked over to the window and looked out. It was very late. A full moon floated above the trees at the back of the center.

A glorious night, the kind made for strolls along the beach, soft murmurs, sweet hunger.

He glanced at the narrow hospital bed and frowned. The doctor had said he'd get out tomorrow. Actually, today, since it was after midnight. What difference could a few hours make?

Finding his clothes, he got rid of the hospital gown and, groaning, slowly but methodically got dressed. Cautiously, he opened the door to his room and stepped outside. The lights were on at the admitting desk but the orderly on duty must have been in the back. There was no sign of anyone.

Going slowly, he walked down the hallway to the front doors. Moonlight flooded the driveway. Conor's eyes lit on his Jeep. He'd last seen it in front of Ed's office. Phil or Dave must have brought it around, figuring he'd need it when he got out.

Way to go, guys.

If the Jeep hadn't been there, he'd have turned around and gone back to his room, been a good little boy and not caused any trouble. Really he would have.

But the Jeep was a sign, or at least he chose to take it as one. A sign that he was really meant to be with Nickie.

That suited him fine. Granted, it was a little tough driving with his arms in the condition they were in, but he could coast part of the way, and besides, there was no traffic to worry about.

He reached the cabin in almost the same time it would have taken him normally. Nickie's car was parked out in front. The lights were still on.

He pictured her still awake, maybe soaking in the tub. The image was vivid enough to banish any physical discomfort he'd been experiencing—and replace it with an entirely different kind.

She had his key, he'd have to knock. No, he wouldn't. The door was open.

He shook his head, making a mental note to warn her to be more careful, and stepped inside.

"Nickie?" he called. He didn't want to take her by surprise. That could be frightening and heaven knew, she'd been through enough.

There was no answer. He tried again. "Nickie?"

Still nothing. For the first time, it occurred to him to hope that she'd opted for a shower. Tired as she was, a long, hot soak might not be a good idea. She could nod off too easily.

He took the stairs to the bathroom two at a time, barely noticing any soreness. "Nickie?"

Nothing, only the sound of the wind moving softly around the cabin and through the nearby pines.

Quickly he went back downstairs and looked in the kitchen. It was empty, as was the living room.

Could she possibly have gone for a walk? It didn't seem likely, but he knew she loved the sea and perhaps she hadn't felt quite ready for bed.

As he was about to head out the back door, he stopped and retraced his steps to the living room. From a drawer in a side table, he withdrew a small box. Inside was his spare revolver. The other one was with the police, waiting his reclaiming.

Outside, he paused and looked carefully in all directions. He could hear nothing except the pounding of the surf. The night remained glorious, but suddenly it had taken on a more sinister edge.

He needed to find Nickie quickly.

The path to the beach was deserted. As it was regularly used by himself, an assortment of deer and various other animals, it was impossible to tell if anyone had been along it recently. At the edge of the sand, he stopped and stood very still, listening.

Far down the beach, he heard a faint sound, not human or animal. A motor.

Somebody was out on the sand in a vehicle. Cursing, Conor ran.

Seated beside Norm in the dune buggy, the gun still held in his right hand and pointed directly at her, Nickie said, "This is crazy. You're making a big mistake."

"No, I'm not," he replied matter-of-factly as he tightened his one-hand grip on the steering wheel. "I

need to get off the island without being hassled. With
you along, McDonnell will have to back off."

"Conor is still in the hospital," she said desperately. "He can't do anything to stop you."

"There were others, I saw them. They came in with
him."

"They left, too, to go to the mainland."

"To talk to Ed." His calm manner fled, replaced by
anger. "He'll tell them everything just to save himself. They'll be after me so fast...."

"You don't know that. He's badly injured. He may
not even live."

"Don't lie to me," Norm said. His voice had turned
shrill. "I know what I know. It's always like this for
me. Everything goes along all right for a while and
then suddenly, it changes. I have to be careful every
second."

Nickie couldn't resist. Never mind the gun or the
fact that he was probably nuts. She had to ask. "If
you're so careful, how did you get mixed up in this
business to start with?"

"Friends," he answered promptly. "I knew them
from the old days and we'd kept in touch." A low
laugh broke from him. It chilled Nickie. "Everything
was so simple back then. We all used, we all sold. It
was no big deal. But a couple of the guys had connec-
tions. I guess that made them take a more long-term
view. Anyway, they've branched out since then, gotten into all sorts of interesting things."

"Like toxic waste dumping?"

"Yeah," he agreed pleasantly, "like that."

She took a deep breath, promising herself that if she got out of this, she'd never take anything for granted again. "It wasn't Ed's idea. You brought him into it."

"That's right. I needed somebody with good organizational skills and no scruples. He fit the bill." Norm paused for a moment. The sand was wet, making tougher going for the buggy. "Or at least I thought he did. Turned out he had no guts."

"For killing Conor?" Rage filled her. How dare this drugged-out refugee from the counter culture think he could end the life of a man as good as Conor and get away with it? Was that really what they were coming to?

"Big mistake," Norm said. "Would have taken care of everything. Now—"

He glanced in her direction and was abruptly silent. All the same, Nickie got the message. She'd have to be as crazy as he was not to.

She wasn't just a hostage for his safe escape. She was the next victim. He had a gun, she had nothing. With odds like that, she'd be smart to stay still and hope for the best.

Smart and dead. It wasn't a good combination.

She took a deep breath, thought of Conor and, turning, hurled herself with all her strength at Norm. Surprise was on her side. He yelled and raised his gun arm to throw her off. The wheel slipped from his left hand just as the dune buggy mounted a rise in the sand.

For a moment the vehicle continued going straight ahead. Norm raised the gun. With no other chance,

Nickie grabbed the wheel and yanked it, hard, to the right.

The buggy swerved on two wheels. A shudder shook it. Halfway up the dune, it slowed, shuddered again, and then began to tip over.

Nickie screamed. If the buggy did flip, it would come straight down on her. She let go of the wheel and without hesitation, threw herself out into the on-rushing darkness.

The sand cushioned her fall. She rolled several yards and came to a stop not far from the waterline. Breathless and shaking, she got to her feet.

Something was coming straight at her, something big, massive against the night. She screamed again and ducked, trying to get away.

"It's okay," Conor said quickly. He took hold of her, his arms closing fiercely around her as though to convince himself she was real. "What in hell happened?"

"Norm..." she said, gasping. "Ed was working for him. The dune buggy—"

There was time for nothing more. A shot rang out, followed by another. Conor threw her to the sand and came down hard on top of her, sheltering her with his body.

He raised his gun and fired.

Epilogue

"Singing like a bird," Phil said. "Now that good old Norm's gone to his reward, we can't shut Mulloney up." He sounded pleased with the situation.

"That's good," Conor said. He was seated in the living room of his cabin talking on the phone, one eye on the paperwork he'd just finished and the other on the door. Nickie had gone for a walk along the beach. He planned to join her.

"So it's all signed, sealed and delivered?"

"Sure is. We can count this one for our side. Speaking of which, there's word going around that you've resigned."

"Only as a marshal. With this case closed, I'd be due for a transfer. I'd rather stick around."

"That coastal survey thing?" Phil asked with a hint of derision. He knew the work was worthwhile. He just couldn't see why Conor would want to do it, at least exclusively.

"Let's just say I want to stay put. You get a chance, come by for a visit. We can do some fishing."

Phil chuckled. "I'll keep that in mind for a few years from now. Maybe by then you'll have come up for air."

"I wouldn't count on it," Conor said. He was smiling when he hung the phone up and flipped the folder shut. Moments later, he was out the door.

Nickie stood staring at the waves. She was well loved, well rested, even well fed. By all rights, she should have been utterly content.

Edward Harper had said as much when they spoke that morning. "That's wonderful, darling girl, he sounds terrific. By all means enjoy yourself. Oh, and when do you think we might talk about the new book?"

Reality was all well and fine so far as Edward was concerned, but it was romance that truly counted. Especially the kind that could be put down on paper.

A low sigh escaped her. It was so much simpler in books. Conor was an absolutely wonderful lover, friend, companion, but everything had happened so quickly. She was just a little afraid that they still didn't really know each other in all the ways that counted.

The whole idea of commitment was daunting. What if they made a mistake? What if they really couldn't get along?

She lived a good part of her life spinning fantasies. He was a hard-core realist. What if that turned out to be a gap they couldn't bridge?

What if neither of them could live up to the other's hopes, dreams, expectations? All those books she'd written, all those happy endings, without even realizing it, she'd set impossibly high standards.

But Conor wasn't one of her heroes. He was a real flesh-and-blood man. She couldn't expect him to be anything else. That would be silly, childish, foolishly, hopelessly romantic.

She just had to come to terms with that. Had to put aside the extravagant, quixotic notions of her stories and settle for what life really had to offer.

Hoofbeats sounded along the sand. She turned, surprised, and raised her hand to shade her eyes from the sun. Sighting down the length of the beach, she caught her breath.

A magnificent black stallion was galloping toward her. The surf sprayed up beneath glistening hooves. On his back, a rider sat with easy grace, his big, muscled body moving perfectly with the horse.

Conor.

Dimly, she remembered that he rode. There was a stable on the island. It stood to reason that he might keep a horse there.

Yet for all that, her heart beat heavily. He was a glorious figure in black riding breeches and a white shirt open at the collar, the thick mane of his hair gleaming, and a look in his eyes that—

Was remarkably like the look Baron Padraic had given his lady right before he scooped her up and carried her off to—

The stallion came to a halt beside her. Conor smiled down. "Care for a lift?" he asked.

Nickie hesitated. Reason told her that this was no more than a coincidence. He'd been in the mood for a ride and had come down to join her on the beach. That was all.

Except that he *had* read her books.

She smiled back, unrestrainedly, joy surging in her. "Which way are you going?" she asked.

"Home," he said, and reached for her.

Home to the cabin beside the sea. To the white house on the hill. To love and laughter, promises and dreams, reality and romance.

Home. At last.

* * * * *

HE'S AN

AMERICAN HERO

He's a cop, a fire fighter or even just a fearless drifter who gets the job done when ordinary men have given up. And you'll find one American Hero every month, only in Intimate Moments— created by some of your favorite authors. Look at what we've lined up for the last months of 1993:

October: GABLE'S LADY by Linda Turner—With a ranch to save and a teenage sister to protect, Gable Rawlings already has a handful of trouble...until hotheaded Josey O'Brian makes it an armful....

November: NIGHTSHADE by Nora Roberts—Murder and a runaway's disappearance force Colt Nightshade and Lt. Althea Grayson into an uneasy alliance....

December: LOST WARRIORS by Rachel Lee—With one war behind him, Medevac pilot Billy Joe Yuma still has the strength to fight off the affections of the one woman he can never have....

AMERICAN HEROES: Men who give all they've got for their country, their work—the women they love.

IMHERO6

OFFICIAL RULES • MILLION DOLLAR SWEEPSTAKES
NO PURCHASE OR OBLIGATION NECESSARY TO ENTER

To enter, follow the directions published. **ALTERNATE MEANS OF ENTRY:** Hand print your name and address on a 3"x5" card and mail to either: Silhouette "Match 3," 3010 Walden Ave., P.O. Box 1867, Buffalo, NY 14269-1867, or Silhouette "Match 3," P.O. Box 609, Fort Erie, Ontario L2A 5X3, and we will assign your Sweepstakes numbers. (Limit: one entry per envelope.) For eligibility, entries must be received no later than March 31, 1994. No responsibility is assumed for lost, late or misdirected entries.

Upon receipt of entry, Sweepstakes numbers will be assigned. To determine winners, Sweepstakes numbers will be compared against a list of randomly preselected prizewinning numbers. In the event all prizes are not claimed via the return of prizewinning numbers, random drawings will be held from among all other entries received to award unclaimed prizes.

Prizewinners will be determined no later than May 30, 1994. Selection of winning numbers and random drawings are under the supervision of D.L. Blair, Inc., an independent judging organization, whose decisions are final. One prize to a family or organization. No substitution will be made for any prize, except as offered. Taxes and duties on all prizes are the sole responsibility of winners. Winners will be notified by mail. Chances of winning are determined by the number of entries distributed and received.

Sweepstakes open to persons 18 years of age or older, except employees and immediate family members of Torstar Corporation, D.L. Blair, Inc., their affiliates, subsidiaries and all other agencies, entities and persons connected with the use, marketing or conduct of this Sweepstakes. All applicable laws and regulations apply. Sweepstakes offer void wherever prohibited by law. Any litigation within the province of Quebec respecting the conduct and awarding of a prize in this Sweepstakes must be submitted to the Régies des Loteries et Courses du Quebec. In order to win a prize, residents of Canada will be required to correctly answer a time-limited arithmetical skill-testing question. Values of all prizes are in U.S. currency.

Winners of major prizes will be obligated to sign and return an affidavit of eligibility and release of liability within 30 days of notification. In the event of non-compliance within this time period, prize may be awarded to an alternate winner. Any prize or prize notification returned as undeliverable will result in the awarding of that prize to an alternate winner. By acceptance of their prize, winners consent to use of their names, photographs or other likenesses for purposes of advertising, trade and promotion on behalf of Torstar Corporation without further compensation, unless prohibited by law.

This Sweepstakes is presented by Torstar Corporation, its subsidiaries and affiliates in conjunction with book, merchandise and/or product offerings. Prizes are as follows: Grand Prize—$1,000,000 (payable at $33,333.33 a year for 30 years). First through Sixth Prizes may be presented in different creative executions, each with the following approximate values: First Prize—$35,000; Second Prize—$10,000; 2 Third Prizes—$5,000 each; 5 Fourth Prizes—$1,000 each; 10 Fifth Prizes—$250 each; 1,000 Sixth Prizes—$100 each. Prizewinners will have the opportunity of selecting any prize offered for that level. A travel-prize option, if offered and selected by winner, must be completed within 12 months of selection and is subject to hotel and flight accommodations availability. Torstar Corporation may present this Sweepstakes utilizing names other than Million Dollar Sweepstakes. For a current list of all prize options offered within prize levels and all names the Sweepstakes may utilize, send a self-addressed, stamped envelope (WA residents need not affix return postage) to: Million Dollar Sweepstakes Prize Options/Names, P.O. Box 4710, Blair, NE 68009.

The Extra Bonus Prize will be awarded in a random drawing to be conducted no later than May 30, 1994 from among all entries received. To qualify, entries must be received by March 31, 1994 and comply with published directions. No purchase necessary. For complete rules, send a self-addressed, stamped envelope (WA residents need not affix return postage) to: Extra Bonus Prize Rules, P.O. Box 4600, Blair, NE 68009.

For a list of prizewinners (available after July 31, 1994) send a separate, stamped, self-addressed envelope to: Million Dollar Sweepstakes Winners, P.O. Box 4728, Blair, NE 68009.

Silhouette Books has done it again!

Opening night in October has never been as exciting! Come watch as the curtain rises and romance flourishes when the stars of tomorrow make their debuts today!

Revel in Jodi O'Donnell's STILL SWEET ON HIM—
Silhouette Romance #969
...as Callie Farrell's renovation of the family homestead leads her straight into the arms of teenage crush Drew Barnett!

Tingle with Carol Devine's BEAUTY AND THE BEASTMASTER—
Silhouette Desire #816
...as legal eagle Amanda Tarkington is carried off by wrestler Bram Masterson!

Thrill to Elyn Day's A BED OF ROSES—
Silhouette Special Edition #846
...as Dana Whitaker's body and soul are healed by sexy physical therapist Michael Gordon!

Believe when Kylie Brant's McLAIN'S LAW—
Silhouette Intimate Moments #528
...takes you into detective Connor McLain's life as he falls for psychic—and suspect—Michele Easton!

Catch the classics of tomorrow—*premiering* today—
only from ▼ *Silhouette*

ROMANTIC TRADITIONS

Marriages of convenience, secret babies, amnesia, brides left at the altar—these are the stuff of Romantic Traditions. And some of the finest Intimate Moments authors will bring these best-loved tales to you starting in October with ONCE UPON A WEDDING (IM #524), by award-winning author Paula Detmer Riggs.

To honor a promise and provide a stable home for an orphaned baby girl, staunch bachelor Jesse Dante asked Hazel O'Connor to marry him, underestimating the powers of passion and parenthood....

In January, look for Marilyn's Pappano's FINALLY A FATHER (IM #542), for a timely look at the ever-popular secret-baby plotline.

And ROMANTIC TRADITIONS doesn't stop there! In months to come we'll be bringing you more of your favorite stories, told the Intimate Moments way. So if you're the romantic type who appreciates tradition with a twist, come experience ROMANTIC TRADITIONS—only in

SIMRT1

INTIMATE MOMENTS ®
Silhouette ®

Next month, don't miss meeting the
Rawlings family of New Mexico.
You'll learn to love them!

Look for

Linda Turner's exciting new miniseries.

Look for GABLE'S LADY (IM #523),
October's American Hero title.

And look for his siblings' stories as the exciting
saga continues throughout 1994!
Only from Silhouette Intimate Moments.

What a year for romance!

Silhouette has five fabulous romance collections coming your way in 1993. Written by popular Silhouette authors, each story is a sensuous tale of love and life—as only Silhouette can give you!

Three bachelors are footloose and fancy-free...until now.
(March)

Heartwarming stories that celebrate the joy of motherhood.
(May)

SILHOUETTE

SUMMER Sizzlers

Put some sizzle into your summer reading with three of Silhouette's hottest authors.
(June)

Take a walk on the dark side of love—with tales just perfect for those misty autumn nights.
(October)

Silhouette
Christmas
Stories

Share in the joy of yuletide romance with four award-winning Silhouette authors.
(November)

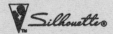

A romance for all seasons—it's always time for romance with Silhouette!

PROM93

TAKE A WALK ON THE
DARK SIDE OF LOVE WITH

October is the shivery season, when chill winds blow and shadows walk the night. Come along with us into a haunting world where love and danger go hand in hand, where passions will thrill you and dangers will chill you. Silhouette's second annual collection from the dark side of love brings you three perfectly haunting tales from three of our most bewitching authors:

Kathleen Korbel
Carla Cassidy
Lori Herter

Haunting a store near you this October.

Only from 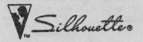 where passion lives.

Fifty red-blooded, white-hot, true-blue hunks from every State in the Union!

Beginning in May, look for MEN MADE IN AMERICA! Written by some of our most popular authors, these stories feature fifty of the strongest, sexiest men, each from a different state in the union!

Two titles available every other month at your favorite retail outlet.

In September, look for:

DECEPTIONS by Annette Broadrick (California)
STORMWALKER by Dallas Schulze (Colorado)

In November, look for:

STRAIGHT FROM THE HEART by Barbara Delinsky (Connecticut)
AUTHOR'S CHOICE by Elizabeth August (Delaware)

You won't be able to resist MEN MADE IN AMERICA!